CASSIE MINT

Practice Makes Perfect
The Complete Series

BLACK CHERRY
PUBLISHING

First published by Black Cherry Publishing 2024

Copyright © 2024 by Cassie Mint

This novel is entirely a work of fiction. The names, characters and incidents portrayed in it are the work of the author's imagination. Any resemblance to actual persons, living or dead, events or localities is entirely coincidental.

Cassie Mint asserts the moral right to be identified as the author of this work.

First edition

ISBN: 978-1-915735-63-8

*This book was professionally typeset on Reedsy.
Find out more at reedsy.com*

Contents

I

Kissing Lessons

Description

He's supposed to teach me about the universe.
I'm mostly trying to get in his pants.

My whole family thinks I'm dumber than a bag of rocks. Just 'cause I like makeup tutorials and wearing pretty clothes, they assume I'm a prize bimbo. When it comes to my college Physics class, I tell them I'm good—but they go ahead and hire a tutor anyways.

Well, joke's on them. Because I understand Physics just fine, but this stern older grad student? I've got plenty of questions about *him*.

And I don't need his quiz prep—not for one minute.

But there are plenty of other things he could teach me…

Lane

❦

O kay, I'll admit it: I came into this tutoring session with a bad attitude. Because after days, weeks, no— *months* of telling my parents that everything is fine, that my grades really are good, they went ahead and hired me a Physics tutor anyway.

A tutor! Like I must be lying. Like there's no possible way I could keep up with these college classes, and surely, given how blonde I am, I must need all the help I can get.

Jerks.

In reality I'm near the top of my class, but do they believe that? No, because girls who wear pink and style their hair can't *possibly* rub two brain cells together. Even though I lived in their house for the first eighteen years of my life, it's not credible.

Bah.

"Latte for Kennedy!"

Scowling at the coffee shop door, I slump down in my chair. All around me, spoons clink against china and conversation

4

hums.

The Brainy Bean is always busy, but it's lunchtime on a Thursday and the place is rammed wall-to-wall with Kephart College students. Steam fogs the big glass windows. Flustered professors check their watches in line by the counter, while student athletes sprawl around tables together, talking loudly about their last game, last carb, last kegger.

Other tables are quieter with students hunched over laptops, buried in their noise-canceling headphones as they tap-tap-tap away at their essays. Plates hold nothing but muffin cases and crumbs.

And me? I'm cupping my own hot mug, glowering at the Brainy Bean doorway like a sulky teenager. I picked the table over in the far corner, tucked against the wall by the noticeboards.

Whoosh. Thwick.

Every time the automatic doors open and close, a breeze drifts across the busy coffee shop and ruffles the fliers pinned on the boards above my head. And every time, I grind my teeth a little harder, waiting for whichever killjoy tutor my parents have hired to tell me that I'm dumb.

Where did they even find this guy? *Ambrose Brent.* With a name like that, they must have dug him up from the nearest graveyard. Bet he lives above a funeral parlor. Bet he hates sugar and fun. Bet he—

"Lane Rhodes?"

A deep voice sounds by my shoulder, making me jump and slosh coffee over the rim of my mug. When I spin around, a tall, lean man stands beside me, frowning slightly at the mess I've made.

His dark hair is rumpled, and tortoiseshell glasses perch on

5

his hawkish nose. He's wearing a dove gray button-down shirt tucked into dark pants, and the open collar shows the hollow of his throat.

"Yes?" I squeak, my bad attitude evaporating like the morning dew.

Because… oh my god. My tutor is *hot*. My parents hired me a hottie.

This is hilarious.

Ambrose Brent meets my eyes for a split second, thick eyebrows spearing down in disapproval. Then he's off, striding across the cluttered coffee shop to gather a stack of napkins. A leather satchel bumps against his hip as he goes.

Biting my lip against a grin, I watch him return. It's like watching a gorgeous, oblivious nerd on a catwalk.

"Here." Ambrose Brent, tutor hottie extraordinaire, flings the napkins onto our table. They stain with coffee as soon as they make contact, wrinkling and soaking up fluid, and if I press my lips any harder together, my whole mouth will disappear. "You should be more careful next time."

"And *you* shouldn't sneak up behind people." My knee jiggles under the table, and oh wow, I can't tear my eyes away from this guy. Everything about him is a work of art. His cranky scowl; the carved lump of his Adam's apple; the pale, corded forearms revealed by his rolled sleeves. The sparkling lenses of his glasses and the small mole on his left wrist.

And the deep, resonant voice that scolds me: "There is a door right behind you."

Don't smile. Don't smile.

"But the main entrance is over there."

"You do understand that two doors can work at once? It doesn't break any rules of nature."

Losing my battle at last, I beam at my new tutor. "Don't you want coffee?"

His gaze flicks to my mug, narrows at the frothy concoction staining the pile of napkins, then turns to the counter and—shifts. Softens.

Ambrose Brent stares at that coffee counter with unbridled longing, like a Shakespearean suitor gazing up at his lover's balcony. His chest rises and falls on a deep breath, like he's sucking the scent of roasted beans into his lungs. His pupils expand behind those polished glasses, and lord, this man *wants*.

But then he clears his throat and drops into the chair opposite mine, all business again. Long, quick fingers clear up the damp napkins, wiping down the table and piling them along one edge like a sandbank.

"No, I had one earlier. Do you have your notes for this semester?"

After that little display? After he practically drooled all over the Brainy Bean floor? *I'm* jonesing for another caffeine fix after that, and I've still got half a mug to drink.

"You can have more than one coffee, you know. It doesn't break any rules of nature."

Ambrose's jaw hardens, and he unfolds a sleek laptop, not bothering to answer. The laptop hums gently, waking at the brush of fingertips over its keys.

My own laptop is wedged in my backpack, ancient and heavy and slow. There's no point in slamming the horrible thing down on this table—even if there was room, which there's not—because by the time I get it to boot up, our session will be over, and we'll both be old and gray.

"So," my new tutor says. Hazel eyes pin me to the spot, magnified slightly by those glasses. "Astrophysics."

"Astrophysics," I agree.

Do my parents realize what they've done? Do they know that they've paid for the biggest distraction of my college career so far? Seriously: have they *seen* this guy?

"Let's discuss the Big Bang," Ambrose says.

I lean forward, propping my chin on one hand. "Oh, yes. Let's."

Ambrose

It is far too hard to concentrate when every breath I take is laced with the scent of roasted coffee beans. Far too hard to think at all in here, surrounded on all sides by temptation, with the constant thump of china mugs against tabletops drumming out a sinful rhythm.

As our session ticks away, a caffeine withdrawal headache creeps its fingers around my skull and *squeezes*, urging me with its vise-grip to crack and go to the counter already.

To cave and order a large black coffee with an extra shot. To plant myself face-first in a bucket of caffeine and wallow around in it like a pig in mud, groaning with relief.

Meanwhile my new student chatters away about relativity, the last dregs of her drink going cold in her mug, wasted.

Wasted. My nostrils flare as I suck in a ragged breath.

Which drink did she get? Some sugary monstrosity, no doubt, with an extra shot of flavored syrup and a twirled head of whipped cream. An insult to coffee beans everywhere. Lane is clearly that type. She's too perky for it to have been decaf, so at least there's that—

"You look ready to suck the spilled latte out of those napkins." Lane smiles and tilts her head, glossy blonde curls brushing against her shoulders. My new student is the Marilyn Monroe of this concrete campus, and the Physics department must descend into chaos whenever she's near. "Are you sure you don't want one? You've held off for twenty minutes now."

Hidden by my laptop, my fist squeezes until my knuckles creak. Am I that obvious? That pathetic?

No, I will not break. Not here. Not now.

Not in front of *her*.

"I'm sure. Tell me about space weather, please."

"But—"

"The weather, Lane."

"I'm just—"

"I know you understand this." Pinching the bridge of my nose, I gust out a sigh. Hell, even my *eyeballs* ache. "Believe me, it is painfully obvious that this session is pointless for both of us, but humor me. Tell me about space weather, so I can charge your parents for this hour with a clear conscience."

Lane blinks at me, straightening in her chair. She's wearing a strappy pink sundress, with a knitted cream cardigan bunching around her slender shoulders. Her blue eyes are wary, scanning me for signs of a lie.

"You know I understand this," Lane repeats slowly. She grips the edge of the table, like she's holding on for balance.

"Yes, obviously." I have many flaws, but I'm not an idiot. "Why on earth did you tell your parents you needed help?"

"I *didn't*." An agitated flush creeps over Lane's cheeks, and her grip tightens on the table until the tips of her fingers go white. "I told them I understood everything just fine, and to trust me for once."

There's a beat of silence between us, which the clamor of the coffee shop rushes in to fill. Hissing steam, scraping chairs, clanging cups. The ring of the register.

My chest is tight. Is that a new symptom of caffeine withdrawal? How troubling.

"Yet here we are," I say at last, not sure what else to say. Dealing with complicated *feelings* has never been my forte, and Lane Rhodes clearly has a metric ton of family baggage.

"Yep. Here we are." Lane sighs and slumps back, suddenly glum. "Maybe if you tell them everything's fine, they'll listen to you."

"Perhaps."

"I doubt it though." Lane smiles, without humor. "They'll think I sweet-talked you into saying that. Seduced you with my womanly wiles."

Womanly—what?

My fingers blur over my laptop keyboard, and I clear my throat as I type, my face suddenly hot. Is it just me, or is the Brainy Bean an inferno today? Must be all the bodies coming in and out, simmering with student hormones. Plus the steam and the spring sunshine beating down on the glass windows. And this shirt.

"I'm emailing your father now."

Lane rolls her eyes and finally, *finally*, tips back the last dregs of her drink. Thank god. Her mug thumps against the table, and the pink tip of her tongue chases a bead of coffee from her lower lip. It's an effort to stay leaning back in my chair, like I wouldn't desperately love to lunge forward and lick that bead away myself.

For the caffeine, of course.

"Don't feel bad about taking his money when he insists you keep tutoring me." Lane prods the napkins into a neater line, her nails painted mint green. "He could believe me any time, but he won't. Even when I show my parents my grades each semester, they assume I must have gotten lucky somehow. Flirted with the professors, or coaxed another student into writing my papers. No way could I have used my brain. God forbid."

My fingers go still on the keys. My cursor winks at me from the laptop screen, my cranky email half-drafted. "I don't understand. Why don't they believe you?"

Lane points to her curled blonde hair, like that's a reasonable answer. It's really not.

"But it would actually be far more devious to cheat your way into good grades."

"I know."

"Even that would require a lot of cunning."

Lane breathes a laugh. "Yeah."

"They're your family. You grew up with them, right? Surely they must know you better..."

Too late, I trail off, finally noticing the pinched expression on my student's face. Lane Rhodes may be a beauty, she may look like some 1950s pin up model wandered into the Brainy Bean, but when her shoulders curl in and her chin drops, she looks tired and completely human.

Christ. I'm an ass sometimes.

"Space weather." Slapping my laptop closed, I leave the email half-written. I'll get to it later, when there's no sad, gorgeous coed wilting before my eyes. "Tell me everything you know, and don't bother trying to half-ass it. I *know* you know a lot."

Lane inhales sharply and raises her chin. Blue eyes flash at me, defiant.

Then my new student launches into a perfect answer, and I fight to focus on each word—never mind the coffee scent, and the clink of mugs, and all the other… distractions.

Lane

❧

We meet for our second session on a picnic blanket in the local park. It's a bright, sunny day, with a strong breeze that keeps tugging on the blanket edges and flipping the pages of my textbook. The park bustles with college students napping off hangovers and playing hacky sack; young families trundling strollers along the paths; old folks chatting on benches. Seagulls shriek overhead, and this close to the sea, the air tastes like salt.

Don't judge me too much, but: I got here early. Came here twenty minutes ago, all so I could drape myself over the picnic blanket and tuck my lilac dress gracefully beneath my legs so it doesn't flap in the breeze. I wanted to check my makeup in my compact mirror and pop a breath mint, then draw in a deep breath and hold it for the count of five, my heart tip-tapping madly in my chest.

See, Ambrose Brent has lived rent free in my brain for the last seven days, and... I'm *nervous.* I'm actually nervous to see the cranky grad student; so on edge that I barely slept last night.

I spent hours and hours tossing and turning, more restless and wired than when I took the SATs, with Ambrose's deep voice reverberating in my brain.

I know you understand this. I know you understand this. I know you understand this.

Did he email my parents?

Did he hate our last session?

Did he ever get another coffee? I need to know!

Sighing, I shift on the pink and white checked blanket and squint at the park entrance. Food packets crinkle beside me, and I bite my lip, second guessing the grapes and mini cupcakes.

Is this too date-like? What if I scare Ambrose off? Mom and Dad would have a field day. They'd finally have their evidence: Lane Rhodes caught attempting to *romance* her tutor, shamelessly using her body instead of pretending to have a brain. Busted.

"You look how I feel."

Appearing from nowhere, Ambrose settles on the blanket beside me. His frown skims over the snacks and two bottles of pink lemonade I brought, and his leather satchel thumps on the grass beside him, straining with books and his fancy laptop.

"And how do you feel?" I ask.

"Irritated." A faint smile passes over his handsome face—a private one, just for me.

"Did anything annoy you in particular?" My eyebrows raise as Ambrose tosses a grape easily into his mouth. There's barely any room with both of us on this picnic blanket, like a life raft in a sea of green grass. "Or is grumpy your standard setting?"

"Both." There's that smile again, here and gone quicker than a blink, before Ambrose sobers. "I emailed your parents and told them you don't need assistance. They insisted that I keep tutoring you every week anyway."

Yup.

I knew that's what they'd say, knew it down to my bones, and it still makes my throat tighten. Swallowing hard, I fight to keep my voice even. "Told ya."

Scowling, Ambrose tosses another grape into his mouth. He chews slowly, thoughtfully, the breeze tousling his dark hair, gazing across the park at a young family playing on the swings. The kid is squealing, begging to be pushed higher, while the parents laugh together over some shared joke. Sunlight sparkles on my tutor's glasses.

Ambrose sighs. "It's bullshit."

My pink lemonade hisses, the lid cracking open. I sip before I speak, tart sweetness spreading over my tongue. "It definitely is."

"But..." Ambrose glances over at me quickly, his expression unhappy. "I'm a grad student, Lane. I know you don't need the help, but if your parents are insisting... I could use the money."

Yeah, I get that. I'm a student too, after all, with a work-study job in the science library and a diet heavier in instant noodles than nature intended. There's no need for Ambrose to be embarrassed, not about this. If my parents want to waste their money, let them.

Still, my shrug is more casual than I feel. "So keep tutoring me. I'm sure we can figure out *something* you can teach me, Ambrose Brent."

Oh my god, is that a blush?

It is!

My stern tutor *blushes,* looking away while his fingers pluck at the blanket. An answering warmth tingles low in my belly, and I push myself to sit up, inspiration striking like lightning.

Ambrose busies himself with my textbook, flicking through to find us a chapter, his hands lean and strong and so much bigger than mine. The breeze flaps his shirt against his body— a moss green button-down that plasters against his muscles with each press of wind. Watching him, my mouth is so, so dry.

And oh, I have a plan, and it's too perfect. Too delicious.

I know *exactly* what Ambrose Brent can teach me.

* * *

"There's a coffee cart over there." Forty minutes later, our hour is nearly up. Ambrose has quizzed me on three chapters, tossing questions about asteroids, comets and gravity in my direction, then nodding with satisfaction each time I bat them back with a solid answer. He's sitting less stiffly than when he first arrived, legs stretched out long and crossed at the ankle, propped up on one elbow to read.

It's *intimate*. Lying with another person on this picnic blanket; feeling the same breeze play over my cheeks that just ruffled Ambrose's hair. The solid warmth of his body near mine has its own special kind of gravity, sucking me closer, and every time Ambrose swigs from his bottled lemonade, I watch his throat shift like it's the best movie ever.

Now Ambrose squints in the direction I'm pointing. "A coffee cart? Where?"

Maybe I shouldn't have said anything, but I'm haunted by the look this man gave the counter in the Brainy Bean last week. The sheer longing in his eyes—it torments me.

Did Ambrose ever get his coffee? Why does he deny himself like that? And would he… would he ever look at *me* that way?

Like he's going insane without me.

Like he might die without a taste.

"By that tree." Food packets crinkle as I sit up, careful to guard my dress against the breeze. "Shall I get us some?"

"I—no." Suddenly flustered, Ambrose tugs at his rolled shirtsleeves. "No, thank you. I've given it up."

"Coffee?" *How?* Most students have more coffee than blood in their veins, and grad students are the worst of all. They're *all* hooked, flocking around the Brainy Bean like caffeine-addicted vampires, barely even human before they get their first sip.

"Yes." Ambrose stops fiddling and turns to me, desperate and haunted. "But it's not going well. Distract me please, Lane."

Oh! Um, sure.

"I want kissing lessons," I blurt, wincing as a red-hot blush stains my cheeks. Bye bye, dignity—it was nice while it lasted. "For our next session."

Ambrose blinks.

"I was going to find a better way of asking. A smoother way."

He blinks again.

"But you wanted a distraction and I panicked." And now I want to die. Where's a handy black hole when you need one? "In my defense, I understand Astrophysics, but I have zero clue about kissing. I've never even tried it. So you'd actually be teaching me something I need to learn, instead of…"

My words trail off weakly.

Ambrose hasn't moved an inch.

My stomach churns as I wait there in silence, shifting awkwardly on the picnic blanket. Eventually, when it's clear it might get dark while we're still out here, staring at each other, I prod his shoulder. He's toned under that shirt.

"Yes," Ambrose says, jolting back to life and shaking his head. "I mean, no. No. Sorry. I can't, Lane... that would be... it would... I couldn't..."

It's his turn to trail off, and I'd curl up into a ball and wither of embarrassment right here—if it weren't for the way his gaze keeps dropping down to my mouth. Ambrose clears his throat, and his tortured eyes dart back to me over and over.

Down to my lips, then away.

To my lips, then away.

To my lips, then to a spot above my left ear.

My uptight tutor doesn't know where to look, but he keeps coming back to my mouth. He's tempted. He's actually tempted.

"Never mind," I say sweetly, offering him another grape. "It was a silly suggestion. We can talk Astrophysics next time too."

Ambrose nods, tugging at his collar. His voice is wrecked. "Good. That's a better idea, Lane."

He doesn't sound happy about it. Smoothing down my dress, I hide a smile.

Ambrose

Albert Einstein was interested in the relativity of time. He noted that time stretches or compresses according to our experience of it—think of the endless minute before a microwave pings, for example, compared to the way a week-long vacation gallops by in a rush.

Privately, I have reached my own conclusion: there is no slower measurement of time than the week between my tutoring sessions with Lane Rhodes.

Kissing lessons. That's what she asked me for.

Kissing lessons. What on earth?

I've barely slept since. Food tastes like cardboard in my mouth; sounds are muffled as I walk across campus and sit in seminars. The week passes in a dull, endless plod of work and study and the campus gym, where I pound out my nightly frustrations on the treadmill, staring dead-eyed at the silent game show playing on the TV screens.

Kissing lessons.

I refuse to believe that Lane Rhodes has not been able to kiss whoever she wants. A young woman like that, with her beauty and intelligence and wit… she could pick anyone. Anyone, and they'd fall to their knees in gratitude.

So has she never wanted anyone before? Is that it?

But why change her mind now? Is this some kind of prank? Or is there someone she likes on campus? Someone she wants to… prepare for?

My feet thud against the treadmill late on Wednesday night, my bones rattling from the impact. Air burns in my lungs. Sweat soaks my t-shirt and trickles down my temples, and I'm pushing too hard, but this makes no sense. *Lane* makes no sense.

Why me?

Why kissing lessons?

The gym is empty except for two male students over by the free weights. They're one-upping each other, chests puffed out with testosterone, talking loudly about drinking and parties and protein and sports. Inhaling sharply, I prod a button on the treadmill to increase the slope.

Need to tune out those idiots.

Need to tune out *Lane*.

Need to stop thinking altogether. Fuck, I'm exhausted. If there were an off-button for my brain, I'd press it in a blink.

The gym is quiet except for the clatter of weights, the faint throb of the radio, and the rhythmic thud of my steps on the treadmill. It smells like sweat and deodorant in here, though someone has thankfully wedged a window open, and a salty breeze rolls in from the nearby coast.

Kissing lessons.

I won't do it. I can't. What kind of arrangement is that? I'm supposed to be a tutor, not a—a gigolo. And Lane would surely come to regret it; she'd feel bad about it and associate those feelings with *me*. I won't set myself up for a fall like that.

Astrophysics is fine. Astrophysics is safe. Tomorrow we'll talk about science, and I'll send Lane back to her dorm unkissed. She'll thank me for it one day.

A dull thud echoes through the gym—a weight dropped to the floor. One of the bros bursts out laughing, and I shake my head slightly, blinking the sweat from my eyes. How long have I been running? An hour? A week?

Is it time to meet Lane yet?

Need to douse myself in an ice cold shower before that time comes, and to give myself yet another strict lecture: *there will be no kissing lessons.*

* * *

Thursday evening in the library is dark and quiet, with the building lit mainly by pools of light from desk lamps. Lines of desks hug the walls around the stacks, where stressed students hunch over their laptops in a sea of snacks, the sickly, pale glow from their screens washing the color from their faces.

It's good that Lane chose here for our third session. A public place. Although—I'd prefer more witnesses to keep me honest. As it is, I find Lane at an isolated desk on the third floor, her workspace a single pool of golden light in the gloom.

Pages rustle and laptop keys tap nearby, so there *are* people on this floor. But they're invisible, wrapped up in their own worlds, sucked into their private study sessions.

"Hi." Lane smiles shyly when I reach her, tucking her blonde hair behind one ear. A pen taps against her notepad. "You came."

My heart slams against my ribs. "Of course I came. Your parents paid me to be here."

Lane's smile falters, and she busies herself shifting books and making room for me. Damn. Sinking down into the seat opposite, I wish I could slap myself without looking insane.

Of course it's not about the money. Or not only that, anyway. The truth is, I'd tutor Lane for free, even though she doesn't need it—I'd take any excuse to bask in the warmth of her presence. But if I say that out loud, she'll wonder what's keeping me coming back, and then her request from last week will be unavoidable. It'll hunker between us on this desk like an invisible demon, prodding us both. *Kissing lessons.*

"Dark energy," I say, levering my laptop open.

Lane nods seriously. "You feel it too?"

Shit. "No, I meant—in the Astrophysics sense—"

"Oh, sure." Lane winks, and my gut clenches in response. She's teasing me. "*That* dark energy. Yeah, let's talk about it."

So we do. I spend the next thirty minutes grilling Lane about dark energy, dark matter, and black holes, and how astrophysicists study that which they cannot see. And while she chatters away, it's impossible not to think about *another* invisible force, pulling the two of us together. A disruption in Earth's field of gravity. The lessons Lane wanted from me instead of this.

"You know what I need?" Lane says after a while, pushing back her chair. She stands and smooths out her blue sundress with a snap of fabric, while I sit and stare at her like an idiot. Is she cold with those bare shoulders? The AC in this library is fierce. "A book."

"A book?" I repeat stupidly.

Seriously. Such an idiot.

"Come on." Lane tucks her chair neatly under the desk and gives me a bright smile. "The Astrophysics section is over there. You can help me look."

Chest thundering, I glance at the library stacks. They're empty and dark.

And private.

"Ambrose."

The soft way she says my name... I'm undone. My chair scrapes back, and my body stands without permission from my brain. I sway on my feet, woozy.

Lane leads me deep into the bookshelves, the fabric of her dress whispering as she walks. I follow silently, with a dry mouth, clenched fists, and stiff limbs, plunging after my student into the labyrinthine stacks.

Of course there's no book.

Of course Lane leads me to the darkest patch of shadow, then turns to me, her blue eyes silvery in the gloom. Of course she grips the front of my shirt, backs herself up to the shelves, and tugs until I'm looming over her. I go easily, moved by a single nudge of her fingertip.

"Just one quick bonus lesson." Lane's hushed words tickle my mouth, because I'm already bending down, already craning my neck, already desperately seeking her lips. She shivers and arches against me, our mouths a hair's breadth apart. "Just once, I promise. Call it a side project."

My blood roars in my ears, and all my common sense is forgotten. All the excellent reasons *not* to do this, not to crowd Lane closer to the stacks and grip the shelves on either side of her head, caging her in—they're long gone.

Distant memories.

Right now, there's nothing but Lane's body heat, and the

warm, minty tickle of her breath, and the coconut scent of her shampoo. Her dress rustles as she shifts.

Someone coughs on the other side of the library. Food packets rustle, and footsteps creak somewhere else in the stacks. Every nerve ending in my body is alive and humming.

"You've really never done this before?" I sound hoarse. Lane's hair brushes my wrist when she shakes her head. "Then why me?"

See, this is the problem with academia. You learn to never let things *be*, never to accept a cosmic gift from the universe. Instead, everything must be picked apart and examined, filtered through the rules of logic, until all the magic has gone.

But Lane won't allow that. She rocks up on her toes, brushing the tip of her nose along my cheek. "Why not you? Don't overthink it, Ambrose."

Well yes, I suppose that's an answer. A deeply unsatisfying one, but an answer all the same. And my chest twists at the thought that it's not *me* Lane wants, just a willing warm body, but I chase after her lips before my pride can get the better of me.

Her breath hitches when our lips meet. Lane stiffens for a split second—then melts against me, moaning softly.

Holy shit.

Warm arms wind around my neck, and I tilt my head, kissing her again.

And again.

And again.

One quick lesson? Hardly. Now that I've started this, I may never stop.

"T-teach me," she gasps between kisses. "Tell me what I'm

doing wrong."

Nothing. Not a single fucking thing. But if I tell her that, our lesson will be over, won't it?

"Tilt your head up." My throat has been sandpapered. "Give me better access."

She does as I say, and immediately I kiss her deeper, tongues sliding together.

"*Mmph.*"

I hope to hell that was a happy sound. Hope this is a good first kiss for Lane; hope it's not ruining her life the way it's ruining mine, because my body is so wired right now that I may never sleep again. If my muscles tense any harder, they could snap bones.

An ankle brushes against my calf as Lane twines around me like ivy climbing a tree trunk. Her breath is hot, and her hands are in my hair, and she's kissing me back fiercely, scraping those pearly teeth over my lip, and I can't think, can't think, can't think.

But I *need* my brain. Need to think straight, damn it, because that's who I am. If I let my body take over, if I'm ruled by my dumbest instincts, then I have no right to be here. No right to teach *anyone*, let alone Lane Rhodes, and fuck, what am I doing?

Tearing my mouth away, I stagger back. Lane thumps awkwardly against the shelves, and a book slams to the library floor, the sound deafening in the quiet. Someone, somewhere, clears their throat.

Lane stares at me with those silvery eyes, her chest heaving.

"There." I take a shaky step away down the aisle. "That's—there. We're done for tonight. Good, uh. Good work today."

Good work today?

Screwing my face up and adjusting my glasses, I stride quickly back through the shelves to our things, then pack up my laptop and sling my bag strap over my shoulder.

But there's no need to act like Lane's chasing me, no need to run away like a coward, because even when I linger for ten seconds, she doesn't appear.

She's horrified, no doubt. Regretting everything.

I knew this was an awful idea.

Lane

~ ✦ ~

K issing lessons with Ambrose Brent is the best idea I've ever had. Oh, he *seems* all cool and aloof, like his toned, lean body is nothing but a vehicle for his massive brain, but now I know otherwise. I have firsthand evidence.

Because on Thursday night, my tutor kissed me like my lips held the secrets of the universe. He squeezed the bookshelves on either side of my head so tight that the wood creaked; he plastered his whole body against mine. And I *felt* it: the unsteady, racing thump of his heart. The wild energy thrumming beneath his neat shirt. Everything.

Whew. It's been three days, and I still haven't caught my breath. At least four separate people have asked me if I'm feeling alright, and whether my fever-bright eyes mean I'm coming down with a cold. Nope, no sickness here—just *need*.

Raging, unsatisfied need for Ambrose Brent and no other man.

Thursday is too far away. I'll never survive that long, not

with this restless tension coiled low in my belly; not with my flushed, over-sensitized skin that goose pimples at the slightest breeze. I've taken more cold showers in the last three days than in my entire life before this week, and it's not enough. It's barely keeping the tingles at bay.

I *need* Ambrose. Not in a few days' time, and not to teach me about Astrophysics. I need more kissing lessons, and I need them now.

Knuckling my forehead on the walk home from a work shift, I call my tutor and press the phone to my ear.

Ambrose picks up on the second ring. "Lane." He sounds worried, his low voice rumbling in my ear. "Are you alright?"

Yes. No.

"I need another lesson." No point in any preamble. I'm an addict, and I'm jonesing for another fix. "Tonight."

A sharp breath crackles down the line. Weaving around a group of students laughing together outside the Brainy Bean, I march across campus like a woman on a mission, my sneakers smacking against the sidewalks.

Never mind my clammy palm where it grips my phone. Never mind the bruised sky, warning of an oncoming storm. I don't draw a breath until Ambrose answers.

"It's Sunday evening."

That's not a no. Raking my free hand through my hair, I tug on a fistful until the roots sting. "Will you come?"

There's a long pause. "To talk about Astrophysics?"

My laugh sounds jittery and weird. "What do *you* think, Ambrose Brent?"

Silence down the line. My thighs burn as I march across campus toward my dorm, pigeons fluttering out of my path at the last possible second.

Then, when I'm ready to fling my phone overarm into the nearest trash can: "...Alright. Where?"

Oh, thank god.

I rattle off my address, and Ambrose repeats it back to me, his tone crisp. The line beeps as it goes dead, and I don't know if I want to laugh or scream or run down the street whooping.

But I do know I want a shower before he arrives.

An icy cold shower, and five minutes with my fingers to get this crawling *need* under control. Otherwise I'll pounce on my tutor like a maniac.

Clutching my phone in my clammy palm, I speed up into a jog, dress swishing around my legs.

* * *

It occurs to me the second I get home: college dorms are not exactly glamorous. The music blasting from three different open doors; the laughter spilling from the common area; the steam wafting from the shared bathroom. Someone's dropped a single clean sock from their laundry, and it lies in the middle of the corridor carpet, forlorn.

When I burst through our door, my roommate Eden blinks at me from her side of the room. She's cross-legged on her bed, surrounded by paper handouts for some class, headphones looped around her slender neck.

"Where's the fire?" she asks.

Steam curls from a bowl on her nightstand—beef flavored instant noodles. Oh god, I have zero right to kick her out, but if I don't get some alone time with Ambrose, I might burst into tears.

"Sorry," I say, standing awkwardly in the doorway and

squeezing the doorknob. "Sorry. This is such a jerk thing to ask, especially when you're eating, but... my tutor is coming over, and I... we need..."

Eden arches one eyebrow. She's my opposite in a lot of ways: tall, beanpole slim, with long dark hair nearly down to her waist. But we clicked at our very first meeting, and I seriously won the roommate jackpot with this girl.

"Some alone time?" she prompts.

"Yes. Please. Sorry. You're the best."

"Mhm." Long legs unfold and Eden gathers her papers together, smirking at me from behind the curtain of her dark hair. "I'll clear out, but on one condition."

Anything. "Yeah?"

"You give me all the details later." Eden winks as she slides off the bed, papers clutched in one hand. She scoops up her ramen bowl with the other. "You know, I think you're onto something with these *lessons*. I should find a tutor of my own. I can't even speak to the guy I like without freezing up."

She pauses, frowning at the carpet, and I fight the urge to hurry her along. My roommate's already clearing out of here; the least I can do is listen when she confides in me.

"But you seem so confident."

Eden snorts. "In *here*, sure. But I know you, and I know all the girls in this dorm. Out there... around this guy..."

Men are a different beast, that's for sure—but most of them aren't worth stressing over. Not like Ambrose.

"You'll figure it out," I say, "when you meet someone you really like. Things will click, and everything will flow easily between you, I promise."

Eden looks troubled. She tears her gaze away from the carpet with a sniff. "Yeah, right. Okay, um... text me when you're done?"

"I will. Thanks, Eden."

"Sure."

The door clicks shut behind her, and I stare around our room in a daze. The two of us aren't sloppy, but we're not neat freaks either, and I spend the next five minutes shoving sweatshirts in hampers, tugging bed covers straight, opening the window and spritzing air freshener around. I tidy and fret like a madwoman, then remember too late that I need to shower, and dash to the bathroom in a panic.

When I come back, Ambrose Brent leans against the wall outside my dorm room, looking so out of place in his button-down navy shirt that it's almost funny. He raises an eyebrow as I hurry toward him, dressed in nothing but jersey shorts, a loose white t-shirt, and shower sandals that smack against my soles.

"Sorry." Scrubbing at my damp hair with a towel, I let us into my room. "Hi. Come in."

Silent and looming, Ambrose follows me inside.

Ambrose

Everything about this room screams that Lane is an undergrad, and that I have no business being here. The two twin beds, pushed against opposite walls, each piled with cushions. The band posters papering the walls, the shower caddy Lane sets on her desk, and the wooden shelf above decorated with post it notes about essay deadlines.

Everything about this room says it belongs to two young women on their first adventure out into the world, and that I should turn around and leave.

I'm so much older than Lane—in experience if not in years. Scrubbing a palm down my face, I turn to my student. "How old are you exactly?"

She frowns, tugging a hairbrush through her damp hair. It's darker blonde when it's wet, and the scent of coconut is stronger than ever. My stomach growls. "Twenty one. Why?"

"Because I'm seven years older than you."

"Psh." Lane waves a hand, draping her towel over the back of her desk chair. "That's nothing."

33

"It's *not* nothing. I'm being—irresponsible."

"If only." Lane's teasing smile stops the panic clawing my throat, if only for a moment. I tug at my shirt collar as she speaks, like I need more air. "You don't have to stay, Ambrose, but I really hope you do. We're both adults. We're not doing anything wrong. And besides… I've missed you."

She has?

Seriously?

Christ, I've missed her too. Over the last few days, every errant thought in my head has been about one person: Lane Rhodes. Lane, Lane, Lane.

Following her into those library stacks, while hearing the soft swish of her dress. Crowding her against those shelves, and feeling her heartbeat where her body pressed against mine. The hot slide of her tongue. The nip of her teeth.

Every detail of our time together haunts me.

But that doesn't mean I should make the same mistakes again. I'm supposed to teach Lane about Astrophysics, not… not *that*.

And yet here I am in her dorm room. Here I am, watching her spin the lock on the door, my abs clenching under my shirt. My heart thumps harder. Can she hear it?

Lane is freshly showered, her bare limbs pink and scrubbed. What does her soap smell like? Would she let me close enough to tell?

Thunder rumbles outside the open window, the evening sky clogged with clouds. Goosebumps rise on my arms, and static crackles in the air. This close to the coast, Kephart College gets lashed by plenty of storms, but tonight's looks like a big one.

"We could talk about aliens." The words scrape out of my throat. "The search for extraterrestrial life." That's part of her module, right?

Lane grins. "We could. Or you could teach me more about kissing."

Fuck.

Is it hot in here? It's stifling suddenly, and no matter how I tug at my collar, I can't get any relief.

Lane flicks on her bedside lamp, then crosses to the wall and smacks off the overhead light. The room turns dimmer; more intimate. Cave-like and quiet, with only the sounds of our soft breaths and music seeping through the walls. Rain starts to fall outside, pattering against the windowpane.

"I'm not sure how much else there is to say about kissing."

Or if there is, I'm not qualified to teach it. Because the second Lane's lips met mine in that library, I lost every thought in my head. I should have been more analytical, less lost in the moment, since that's what Lane asked me for: tuition.

Not shameless enjoyment.

"Something else, then," Lane says, her tone light. She sits on the edge of her mattress, bouncing a little, and tilts her head as she watches me. "There must be more to learn. I mean, I can think of a dozen things I'd like to do to you, Ambrose Brent, and ideally do well."

Jesus Christ.

It's not about me.

Need to keep reminding myself of that fact. It's not *me* Lane wants, it's a tutor. This is practice for her. Practice, so that when she meets a man she truly wants, she's ready to blow his unworthy mind.

Can't let myself forget that. Can't let myself get too sucked in, or else the day will come when Lane moves on from our lessons, and my whole world will turn gray.

35

But I can do this. Science is all about keeping an objective distance—keeping the world at arm's length to study it better. I am fully capable of keeping my emotions in check.

"I want to touch you," Lane says suddenly, interrupting the silent battle raging in my head. "Will you let me?"

My head nods unbidden, and my hand tugs out the desk chair. I sit facing the bed. Lane scooches to the edge of the mattress, her bare knees between my own spread legs, and I'm already ruined, ruined, ruined.

"Tell me what I'm doing wrong." I barely hear her soft voice over the pulse thudding in my ears. "Give me corrections, Ambrose. Teach me."

A hand hovers over my chest—then finally, *finally*, makes contact.

All Lane has done is rest her hand over my chest, the sensation muffled by my shirt, and already I'm choking back a groan.

It's been so long. The last three days have been interminable, my thoughts scattered and my mood wild, and the sheer relief when Lane finally touches me again... it takes me by surprise.

It's a jolt, a shock to my system, followed by the blissful spread of calm through my chest. My heartbeat raps against her palm.

Outside the window, thunder rumbles again, and the rain lashes harder. It smells like wet concrete and copper pennies.

"Well?" Lane whispers.

Glancing down at her hand on my chest, I can't resist breaking into a smile. "No notes so far."

Her giggle is so fucking sweet.

Down, down, down her hand trails, my shirt buttons catching against the heel of her palm. Lane strokes a slow, heated

36

path down my chest and stomach, humming at the tensed muscles she can feel through the fabric.

"I like touching you, Ambrose Brent."

And I like being touched—by Lane Rhodes, anyway. I'm like an overgrown house cat, practically purring beneath her stroke. My teeth clench together to keep me from saying anything stupid, and after a long pause of waiting for a reply, Lane sighs and keeps going.

Her other hand rests gently on my knee, then trails slowly up the length of my thigh. And Lane leans closer as she reaches my hip, her cheeks already flushed in the lamplight, until both hands are on my belt buckle.

Lane nibbles on her bottom lip, blue eyes darting away. She's suddenly shy. Unsure. "Um."

Catching her wrists, I move both hands back to my shoulders. "Lesson one: you don't need to rush."

Not if she's not ready. Not if Lane feels as out of control and dangerous as *I* feel right now, like the whole planet has spun off its axis. My student puffs out a breath, and gives me a wobbly smile.

"Okay. I'll keep exploring, then."

And I'll keep dying inside with every touch. Works for me.

Freed from the pressure to get under my clothes, Lane relaxes into her study of me. I'm like a creature in a lab, pinned in place for her observations as she strokes along my upper arms, my elbows, my forearms.

When she crosses from rolled shirtsleeves to bare arms, Lane sucks in a sharp breath. She's not the only one, and when her eyes dart to mine, electricity arcs between us.

Lightning strobes outside, forking through the night sky.

Meanwhile, those small hands are lighting up my nerve

endings like a switchboard.

Pressing her lips together, Lane tugs one of my hands into her lap, and I fight fiercely to ignore the brush of bare thigh against the backs of my knuckles. She rubs both thumbs along the grooves of my palm; measures my wrist with her fingers; squeezes my knuckle joints one by one.

"Men's hands are so funny."

"Oh?"

Lane turns my wrist this way and that, then presses our palms together and measures our hands side by side. Mine is much larger, and my fingers curl over her fingertips, the move oddly possessive.

"They're more... sort of... squared off."

Huh. "I suppose they are."

"No wonder you can lift more stuff."

My mouth twitches. "No wonder."

"The sports guys always act like they're such gods for catching a ball or whatever, but then they're wandering around with hands like dinner plates." Lane shifts on the mattress edge, her eyes sparkling when I laugh. "You know what's *actually* more impressive for men, with hands like these? Detail work."

Couldn't agree more.

And there is some *detail work* I'd dearly love to carry out on Lane Rhodes.

Want to slide my hands under that baggy t-shirt and find the hard beads of her nipples. Want to grip the sides of her body and feel the buried ridges of her ribs. Want to coax those thighs apart and delve beneath those shorts, and show this girl how the tiniest brush of a fingertip, the smallest touch, can make her whole body quiver with sensation.

Instead I sit statue-still as Lane stands and steps closer

between my legs. Even standing, she's barely taller than me, with the flyaway strands of her blonde hair lit up gold by the lamplight. My head tips back so I can watch my student, chest drumming, and she slides off my glasses and places them gently on the desk.

Lane grips my shoulders. She squeezes my collarbone, like she's testing that I'm structurally sound—then she slings one leg then another over my hips, settling her perfect ass in my lap.

Lane gusts out a pleased sigh, her arms winding around my neck.

Oh, Christ.

I crush her closer.

Lane

❧◦❧

O h yeah, here we go. I've found Ambrose Brent's secret button: all I need to do is sit in his lap, and his maddening restraint flies out the window. As soon as my weight settles on him, Ambrose grunts and wraps me in his strong arms, squeezing me against the planes of his chest. He goes from a stern statue to burying his face in my hair, breathing deep like he wants to draw me into his lungs, and I love it, I love it, I love it.

Part of me feared that all this time, Ambrose was humoring me. Going along with my special 'lessons' out of pity or something, but not really into it himself. I tortured myself with that idea—nearly gave up a dozen times already tonight— but I'm so glad I pushed him one last time.

Now I know better. Now I'm *sure* my tutor wants me too, because he's gripping my hips and rolling our bodies together. He's kissing down my throat, his hot breath misting my skin.

"Lane." His low voice reverberates against my skin as he mouths my neck, my jaw, my earlobe. "Christ. Lane. You feel… I could just…"

Whatever Ambrose could *just*, I sure wish he would. Wish he'd throw all caution to the wind outside. Wish he'd rip my clothes off, toss me down onto that mattress, and have his wicked way.

My fingers are clumsy, but I flick his shirt buttons open one by one. When my hands find bare chest, smoothing over his warm bulk, Ambrose's groan vibrates against my palm.

He's hard beneath me. Every time my tutor rocks our hips together, I ride the buried length of him, my belly twisting in response. He *does* want this. So what are we waiting for?

Lightning flashes outside, quickly followed by the rumble of thunder. The storm is closer now, wind howling and tossing handfuls of rain at our cracked window, but this dorm could fly up into the sky Wizard of Oz-style right now and I wouldn't care.

"I want you."

Ambrose grunts at my breathless words, then captures my mouth in a fierce kiss. But when I fumble at his belt again, he plucks my hands away, caging my wrists.

"Not tonight."

Um. *What?* "Why not?"

A warning frown. "Because I said so. Now do you want me to lick your pussy or not?"

Competing instincts war inside me: one big part of me wants to shove off stupid Ambrose Brent's stupid lap and tell him where to shove his stupid, bossy offer. I can't believe he's turned me down *again*. So humiliating.

But the rest of me wants to drape myself on the bed and open my legs and *beg* for his mouth down there, because I desperately need to come, and only this man in the whole world can scratch my itch.

Ambrose scowls at me while I war with myself, one eyebrow raised.

Ugh. Tutors are the worst.

"Fine!" I hop off his lap with terrible grace, splitting the difference between my two instincts: going along with the pussy-licking idea, but with the worst possible attitude. "If you're not too high and mighty for this part, sure. Knock yourself out."

Ambrose barks a surprised laugh. "Lane..."

My shorts and underwear puddle around my ankles, cutting him off with the sight of my bare body. I dressed in such a hurry after the shower, barely threw on any clothes at all, and the only scrap I'm wearing now is my baggy white t-shirt. I shrug that off too and fling it at the wall.

Ambrose should at least see what he's missing. Jerk.

Oh god, why doesn't he want me that way? What did I do wrong?

Buck-ass naked, with my pride hanging by the thinnest of threads, I raise my chin and meet my tutor's eye. "Well? Any notes yet?"

His mouth actually twitches. He finds this funny! I'm gonna kill him. "We could use an attitude adjustment, maybe. But then, some men like brats."

Just like that Ambrose's humor fades—like he hates the mention of other men as much as I do. It sours something inside me; makes me want to cover up with a sheet. Because who cares what other men like? I want to please *this* man, and only this man, for as long as we both shall live.

My heart shrivels in my chest. I'm so screwed.

"Sit on the edge of the bed." Ambrose's voice is gravelly

again, like he swallowed a bunch of sharp rocks. "Lie back, Lane. Spread your thighs."

Lips pressed tight together, I do as he says. The mattress plunks beneath my weight, and the bed sheets are soft against my back.

Ambrose slides off the chair to kneel by the bed, his heated gaze fixed between my legs. I'm so desperate for his touch that I can't breathe, and my stomach muscles are so taut they tremble.

Strong, warm palms cup my knees and nudge me wider. The wind howls outside the window, a small branch crashing against the windowpane before flying away.

"Please." Guess the brat has left the building. All that's left for me to do is beg shamelessly, fingers twisting in the bed covers, staring wide-eyed at my tutor between my legs. I'm propped on my elbows, afraid to blink in case he disappears. "Please, I'm sorry about just now. Please kiss me down there. Please don't change your mind."

The smile Ambrose gives me is achingly soft. It cracks something open deep inside me.

"As if I could. Relax, Lane."

Relax. Yeah, sure, I can do that. No worries.

I mean, I've never had another human being inspect my lady parts before, but totally. I'm cool. At least I showered, right? Ahahaha.

"Christ," Ambrose mutters, glaring between my thighs, and I tense up even more with a squeak.

"Is there something wrong with me? Do I smell weird or something?"

An annoyed glance in my direction. "What? No. No, of course not. I'm just thinking that this is going to haunt me

43

for the rest of my life." Two hands trail up my thighs as my tutor speaks, before settling on either side of my slit. Inhaling sharply, Ambrose draws his hands apart slightly, until my slickest, pinkest parts appear.

I quiver.

"Fuck," he says, eyebrows spearing down. But now that I know his crankiness is a *good* thing, that it's a weird kind of compliment, my cheeks ache from smiling. I shift my hips, wriggling to tease him, and Ambrose gives me a *look* before ducking his head. The waft of warm breath is my only warning. Then—

Thick, dark hair tickles my inner thighs.

His sharp jaw flexes, his eyes falling closed.

And—that *mouth*.

The hot, maddening stroke of his tongue. The scrape of his teeth; the suction of his lips. It's so much sensation, a sudden overload without warning, and I only notice I'm wailing when thunder rumbles again, drowning out the sound. My hips shift restlessly, and Ambrose pins me down then licks me deeper.

Ho-ly. Shit.

Ambrose Brent takes zero prisoners. My stern, uptight tutor is eating me alive, unleashing all his frustrations on the most sensitive parts of my body, and I can't even blame him for the lack of preamble. After all, I've tortured us both for weeks now, teasing and flirting. I've built us up to this, lit the fuse with my own match, and now Ambrose is punishing me for it, his jaw cracking as his mouth works between my thighs.

The heat.

The tingles.

The throbbing pulse in my clit.

I can't—can't *breathe*.

"Oh!"

Ambrose doesn't lift his head, but I *feel* his evil smile curve against me. And I'm squirming, thrashing, but he holds my hips in a merciless grip, chasing me higher and higher with his tongue.

"Please!"

Ambrose slides one palm up my stomach then grips my breast hard, kneading and testing it so possessively that I cry out and arch into his hand.

I *want* him to touch me like that. Like I'm his plaything. His doll.

Shoot, were my parents right about me? Am I nothing more than an empty-headed bundle of hormones? Before that thought can take hold, Ambrose licks inside me, and my brain quietens down again.

"Come for me." His words are desperate, ragged, but he doesn't need to boss me about. Not about this. I'm already hovering on the precipice, my body flooded with heat; already teetering past the point of no return. So when Ambrose sucks hard on my clit, I buck against his mouth with a wild cry, and shuddering waves course through my whole body.

It lasts forever. So much longer than when I bring myself off with my fingers—so long that I wonder distantly whether he's broken me and I'll be stuck coming for eternity.

Then I flop back against the bed, breathing hard, and Ambrose sits up, his chin slick. He snags my towel off the back of the chair and wipes his mouth, then turns to me.

"There. That's lesson two."

I smile, but my giddy heart sinks.

Ambrose

I am the instigator of my own torture. *I* am the reason I know the taste of Lane Rhodes' most intimate, salty-sweet tang; I'm why her breathless cries and whimpers have echoed around my head since Sunday. I'm the reason I haven't slept in days, and I'm the reason my sanity has unraveled.

No one else did this to me. No one forced me to lay my student back on that mattress, or pushed my head between her warm, soft thighs.

Now I'm haunted. Ruined. Going slowly insane.

And I'm late for my tutoring session with Lane in the Brainy Bean.

My legs carry me across campus with long, agitated strides, my satchel banging against my hip. All around me, students sun themselves in the watery spring sunshine. They have no troubles on this cool Thursday.

The sky is calm: not a cloud or a single gust of wind. There's no sign at all of the storm that raged over the weekend—nothing except for the broken branches still strewn across campus, dropped on grassy verges and swept against walls.

That, and the memory of lightning flashing outside Lane's open window, strobing her bare body with light. The rattle of rain against her windowpane; the smell of wet cement and sea brine. The way her moans mingled with thunder.

Fuck.

A pigeon hops out of my way, cooing, and I shake my head and walk faster. There's no use daydreaming about my foolish mistakes now. I need to get to the Brainy Bean before Lane thinks I blew her off.

Fifteen minutes late. I'm *never* late, and I have no excuse today except that I was wrestling with myself endlessly, debating about whether it was more honorable to stay away or turn up. I still haven't decided, but in the end I couldn't bear the thought of Lane sitting there, alone. Waiting.

"Shit." My heart drums in my chest, but not because of the race across campus. No, my heart's been working overtime since the first day I met Lane Rhodes in this very coffee shop. "Shit, shit, shit."

The Brainy Bean's automatic door whooshes open, and I'm hit with a coffee-scented wall of steam. The old caffeine addiction rears its head, squeezes my temples hopefully, but frankly, I have bigger addictions now.

The coffee shop is full, with every table occupied and cluttered with mugs and plates. I scan for a head of blonde curls, barely breathing.

There.

Lane is slumped at a table in the back corner, fiddling sadly with the corner of a napkin. Her shoulders are curved over, and her mouth is down-turned. Even her bouncy hair is limp.

When she glances up and spots me weaving between tables

toward her, it's like the goddamn sun comes out. Blue eyes light up; color glows on her cheeks. Lane sits up straight and hits me with a wide, joyful smile, and—what am I doing? Seriously, what am I doing?

It's been four days since I saw her last. Since we did... *that*.

Why did I wait so long to see this girl again? Who am I fucking kidding?

Chairs scrape as their occupants help shuffle out of my way, and I murmur my thanks but don't look away from Lane. As if I ever could. She's spinning a mug between her palms—something frothy and sweet—but for once I'm not jealous of her drink. I'm jealous of the touch of her hands.

I love her. This new hypothesis rolls through my brain, and finds no evidence to contradict the statement. Not a single damn thing.

I love Lane Rhodes. Obviously.

It's an inconvenient discovery to make in the Brainy Bean, especially when this place is packed with chatting students and rushed professors and college athletes in gym gear, stretching their long limbs in the line at the counter. It's busy and loud in here, filled with an over-caffeinated crowd, but at least it's hot enough to hide the flush on my cheeks.

"Hi." Lane sounds breathless as she shuffles her notebook and coffee mug over to make room. I sink into the chair opposite her, my tongue too leaden to speak.

I'm in love with this girl.

In love with my tutoring student.

In love with someone who's been using me for *practice*.

Christ.

"Did you forget we had a session?" Lane's smiling brightly, not offended at all by my rocking up fifteen minutes late

48

without a word of excuse—though there's an undercurrent of anxiety beneath her words. "I do that sometimes. Mix up the days of the week, I mean. Last month I sat in an empty lecture hall and it took me way too long to realize it was Sunday, not Monday."

Her pen taps nervously on her notepad. Lane nudges my foot with her own beneath the table.

And—hell. I don't deserve this girl. Don't deserve her trying to make me feel better, after *I* was late. Don't deserve her assuming the best of me, and telling an anecdote that makes her seem absent-minded, even when her parents constantly think she's an airhead.

"I…" Clearing my throat, I try again. "I wasn't sure if I should come."

Lane's smile falls. Her foot moves away from mine under the table, and I'm left feeling cold.

She's wearing another sundress—yellow this time, with little embroidered daisies. Her shoulders are bare and lightly freckled, and her pulse thuds at the base of her throat.

"What?" Lane says. "Why not?"

The answer to *that* question feels so painfully obvious that I bark out a laugh. I wave a hand between us, though of course that's no answer at all.

Lane wilts in her seat. Chewing on her bottom lip, she stares at her notepad, scrawled with notes from a different class.

"You don't have to keep seeing me, you know. As my tutor or… anything more. No one's making you, Ambrose."

No, no one's *made* me do any of this: tutor a student who doesn't need help; break my own code to kiss her; fall in love against all my survival instincts. Turn up late today and make everything worse.

49

This is all me.

And I know it makes me the biggest ass in the universe, but a small, bruised part of me rankles when Lane seems so calm about it all. Would it really be so easy for her to end our arrangement?

Would Lane find someone else for her *kissing lessons*? Does she already have someone in mind?

I squeeze the edge of the table until my knuckles ache.

"Just tell my parents you're no longer available," Lane says dully, still staring at her notepad. She's doodling a flower. "They'll insist on finding someone else to tutor me, obviously, but you'll be off the hook. Problem solved."

My chest burns.

Problem solved? Problem *solved*?

"Fine," I grate out. "Good idea. It's probably for the best, anyway. This was becoming a distraction."

And then, only then, does Lane finally glance up—and hit me with the hurt swimming in her big, blue eyes. Tears brim, and her lower lip wobbles.

Fucking hell.

It's a punch to the chest. My thoughts scatter, my lungs freeze, and only my grip on the table keeps me anchored in place, because Lane looks *agonized*. Like this hurts her every bit as much as it hurts me, and how did I not see that before? Why did I assume I'm some lone ranger, completely alone in these feelings? Didn't I feel the hungry way she kissed me? Didn't I feel her shy trust when she lay back for me on Sunday night?

I'm such an ass.

"A distraction," Lane chokes out. "Yes. Okay."

"No, wait—"

She stands up on wobbly legs, grabs her notepad and pen and stuffs them blindly into her backpack. Lane reaches for the mug too, then catches herself before pouring a whole frothy coffee in her bag. Blue eyes blink at me in a daze.

"Um. See you around, Ambrose."

"Lane, hang on a second. Please, just wait—"

She stumbles away from our table to the nearest door, bouncing one shoulder off the wall. Like I've injured her physically as well as dealt an emotional blow.

My own chair screeches over the floor, and I stagger after her, but chairs push back and slow me down.

When I spill through the door onto campus, every hacky-sack player in a ten mile radius rushes to get in my way.

"Lane!"

I'm crowded, jostled, surrounded by stoners and skateboarders and someone pushing a flier into my chest, telling me to come to the drama school's production of Romeo and Juliet. I bat them away, desperately scanning for a head of blonde curls.

"Lane!"

In the distance, she hurries away, dress swishing around her thighs. She disappears around the side of the building—and when I finally break free of this mob and run after her, I round the building to find... no sign.

Breathing hard, I press my knuckles into my chest, then march forward, scanning the different paths Lane could have taken. Nothing.

My student has disappeared into thin air.

I stand rooted in place, ice cold sweat trickling down my back.

Just like that, I've lost her.

51

Lane

❦

It's childish to run away from my problems, I know. Childish to hurry away from Ambrose's calls, refusing to have an adult conversation about the fact that he just tore out my heart and trampled it. And childish to wander into Kephart town and pace the streets for hours, wandering in and out of book shops and thrift stores without buying a single thing, just desperate to keep my body moving and my thoughts away from campus.

This is probably *exactly* what my parents would expect of me. Oh, Lane? Crushing on her tutor then falling apart when he doesn't want her? Of course she'd go shopping to feel better! She has more shoes than brain cells!

Bleurgh.

My phone keeps buzzing in the bottom of my backpack, vibrating against the base of my spine, but I ignore it. I don't need any stern welfare checks from Ambrose Brent, because he made his position completely clear.

This was becoming a distraction.

If only, motherfucker! If. Only.

If I'd haunted Ambrose Brent's thoughts half as much as he haunted mine this week, he would never have called things off so easily.

Clothes hangers slide over the rail as I browse in a third thrift store, metal clinking, and I barely register the brush of fabric beneath my fingers. This is just something to do with my hands; somewhere to point my eyeballs while my insides fall apart. The store smells like dust bunnies and gingerbread, and it's stuffy and warm, but at least it's far from campus.

From Ambrose.

"Looking for a gift?" a white-haired older woman calls to me from the checkout stand, her eyes crinkling kindly behind her glasses. She cocks her head, expectant.

I glance down. I'm in the men's section, flicking through lumberjack shirts.

Awesome.

"Looking for me, actually," I tell the woman, hooking one arm like I'm flexing my non-existent bicep. "Thinking about running into the woods to become a lumberjane."

She clucks with amusement, but now that I say it out loud, that plan is not half bad.

Sure, I have zero upper body strength and get awful hay fever in the summer. Sure, I'm scared of bugs and weird noises at night. But I could totally adapt to the woods! I could learn to swing an ax, I could light campfires, and I could…

No, these shirts are all ugly.

Whatever.

"Thank you," I call to the woman, waving as I leave the store. Maybe I won't run away to the woods, but I'll find *something* to distract me from Ambrose Brent.

* * *

One dumb horror movie later, I'm fast running out of excuses to stay away from campus. My phone stopped buzzing in my bag about an hour ago, and I can't decide if that makes me feel better or worse. Mostly I feel empty, I think.

I get a giant slice of pizza and eat it off a paper plate, standing up outside and squinting out at the hazy pale sea in the distance. Hot cheese burns the roof of my mouth, but I keep chewing, robotic, trying to think of anything except Ambrose Brent.

That calculus test I have coming up.

The full laundry hamper in my room.

The voicemail my parents left me last week, asking with genuine concern how I was 'coping' with my classes.

Anything except narrowed hazel eyes, and that deep voice rumbling down to my bone marrow. Anything except the firm strength of a certain chest beneath my hand, and the way his buttons snagged on the heel of my palm as I stroked down his body, and the red mark his glasses leave on the bridge of his nose.

My heart howls like an abandoned puppy.

Clouds gather overhead as I eat my pizza. Gray and full-bellied, they scud over the town on brisk winds, then hunker down and start spitting rain. Perfect. Cold droplets fleck my cheeks as I chew the last bite of sourdough crust.

A cold breeze gusts through the streets, riffling my sundress, and I fold my plate and napkin with a sigh.

Time to stop running.

Well—*after* I jog back to the dorm, the rain getting heavier and heavier until my sundress is sodden and sticking to my thighs. By the time I burst through the dorm door, strands of my hair are plastered to my cheeks, and I'm breathing hard and shivering like crazy.

Some of the girls fuss over me when they see my drowned rat act, offering to grab towels and boil hot water for tea, but I wave them all off and shuffle to mine and Eden's room, my shoes squelching.

When I push the door open, I fully expect to be hit by the memory of Ambrose in here, pulling up a chair to the bed. Every minute I spend in here these days, it's difficult to think of anything else. What I *don't* expect is to find the man himself, standing awkwardly with his hands shoved in his pockets, while Eden works at her desk with big, boxy headphones on.

As soon as I open the door, Eden turns around and they both speak at once.

"Lane, sweetheart—"

"He insisted on waiting, but I didn't leave him alone in here, I promise."

"What on earth? You're shivering—"

"I can kick him out if you like."

"Here, you need to get warm."

I stand there like an idiot as Ambrose grabs my towel off the back of my desk chair, then crosses the room in three strides and wraps it around my shoulders. He's staring down at me with such fierce concern, fussing over me and squeezing the moisture from my hair with a corner of the towel, and oh god. Oh god.

He doesn't want me.

Does he?

"Where *were* you?" Ambrose says, and he sounds so agonized, I have the weird urge to comfort *him*. "I've been calling and calling."

"Sounds like you should take a hint," Eden says, but I shoot her a wobbly smile past Ambrose's shoulder, trying to reassure my friend. I don't really mind that my tutor kept calling, even if I didn't answer. *Especially* since I didn't answer.

Jeez, I'm as dramatic as the acting students sometimes.

"So, should I..." Eden widens her eyes, then looks pointedly at the door. I shrug helplessly, then nod.

"Please," I say. "I'll make it up to you, I promise."

My roomie gathers up her laptop, her notepad, and her giant mug of coffee. "No need. But I *will* be right down the hall if you need anything."

Those words are directed at Ambrose—a clear threat. It's like a kitten growling at a panther, and I press my lips together to fight a laugh. "Thank you."

As soon as the door clicks shut behind Eden, Ambrose crushes me to his chest, wrapping me tightly in his arms. And I'm soaked through and definitely leaving a huge wet patch on his button-down shirt, but my tutor doesn't seem to care.

"I messed up," he says, pressing the words against the top of my head. His breath is hot and tickly, and I squirm closer, slotting the tip of my icy nose into the hollow of his throat. Ambrose chafes my bare arms, trying to warm me up.

"I'm so sorry, Lane. I thought you weren't serious about me, and I lashed out, trying to protect my ridiculous ego. Of course I don't want this to end. Of course I love you. For goodness' sake, sweetheart, how did you get so cold? Where did you go? No, wait, you don't have to tell me. But fuck, I've been so worried."

Okay, *now* I feel kinda bad for ignoring my phone.

"I just wandered around town for a few hours. I wanted to stay away from campus and forget about... about everything.

56

For a little while. But I got caught in the rain on the way home."

My words are muffled against Ambrose's chest, and his hum reverberates against my chin.

"Your roommate thinks I'm a stalker. I've been waiting here for hours, asking her where you might have gone."

Ha. Oh dear.

"Eden will come around," I say, sounding more sure than I feel. "Once she sees you more often, she'll get used to you."

Ambrose sucks in a breath and goes still. His warm, strong arms cage me in, and his throat bobs as he swallows, and his heart thuds loudly in his chest.

"Does that mean—are you saying—?"

"You do want me, right?" I ask weakly.

"Yes." My tutor bursts back in motion, plastering me even closer. "So fucking much. You have no idea, Lane. From the first time we met, even—"

My insides glow warm. "Me too."

"Yeah?"

I nuzzle his throat. "Yeah."

It's all a blur after that. A shivering, laughing blur, as Ambrose peels me out of my sodden sundress and flings it onto my overfull hamper, then chafes every inch of me with the towel and bundles me beneath my bed covers.

"I need body heat," I say, snaking out an arm to reach for him, but Ambrose is already shrugging off his shirt and dropping it on my cluttered desk. He undresses the way he does everything: with maximum efficiency and barely a flicker of emotion. The glasses are the last to go.

Then he slides into bed with me, and Ambrose Brent is *pure* emotion. Love and need shine out of his handsome face as he rolls on top of me and cages me in with his forearms, kissing me hard and deep and true.

Heat builds and builds, chasing away my shivers until I'm sweating and flushed. The bed springs sing out in a chorus as we kiss and grip and writhe.

"Your bed is shit," Ambrose tears his mouth away to say at one point, rubbing the tip of his nose over my cheekbone. "Next time, stay at my place."

I hook a leg over his hip. "Deal."

Eden would like that better too, I'm sure. But for now, I'm glad my roommate is far away down the hall, because when Ambrose's hard length rubs between my legs... I couldn't stop this for a category five hurricane.

Ambrose

Lane Rhodes is so fucking sweet beneath me, panting and mewling and arching up to kiss me hard, her fingernails clawing hot streaks down my bare back. She's everything I knew she'd be and more, her damp hair spread over the pillows, and it feels odd that the sounds of the dorm are seeping through the walls: other girls' music, laughter and conversation from the common area, the faint smack as someone drops their shampoo bottle in the shower.

Surely there should be angelic choirs singing, or something. Surely it should be just the two of us, marooned on a desert island, with nothing but the shiver of palm leaves and the gentle *hush, hush,* of the waves.

It doesn't matter. Literally nothing could make this moment less meaningful—not even when someone sprints down the hall outside, cackling. It just makes Lane giggle, burying her face in my neck.

So hot.

So soft.

So perfect.

Fuck, I thought I'd lost her. My chest aches at the memory, the sting still not fully healed, and I hitch Lane's thigh higher around my hip, rocking against her. Suddenly so desperate to get *in*.

"We don't have to." My voice is raw. "If you're not ready, or if you just don't want to. Tell me to stop, Lane, and I will."

She cups my face, blue eyes bright and happy once again. "Duh. But I want this. Don't you?"

Oh, please. Lane can *feel* how badly I want her—can feel the bruising hardness of my shaft, my pulse throbbing in the vein, can feel the way my breath hitches every time I glide through her wet folds.

"Don't want to hurt you," I mutter.

Lane kisses my cheek. "You won't. Come on, we can call it another lesson."

My laugh is strangled. "Absolutely not."

Because I don't want to teach her this. I want Lane to respond to my touch completely naturally, following her instincts instead of some made-up script. I want this to be *real*.

When I notch at her entrance, Lane stiffens slightly. Nerves. That's understandable.

"Relax." I kiss her until she melts beneath me again, sinking boneless into the mattress, and then I reach between us to rub at her clit until she's slick and quivering, wetter than the weather outside.

"Please," she whispers.

Only then do I sink into her body.

Slowly, gently. Letting Lane stretch and adjust. Letting her breathe and moan and claw at my back, kicking at my calves with her heels as she gets impatient and urges me on.

In. Out.

We move together slowly at first—grappling tight, kissing hard. Her channel is hot and tight and so perfectly wet that I slide in and out easily, never mind that it's her first time.

In. Out.

Lane bucks her hips and grips fistfuls of my hair. My teeth scrape her bottom lip, and I taste the coppery bloom of blood, but she doesn't mind. She groans and pulls me deeper.

Time passes, but it could be minutes or hours. Rain lashes the closed window, and it's dark outside, but we're cocooned here in this muggy warmth. The room smells like sex, and wet noises sound where our bodies meet, and it's earthy and perfect and real.

"A–Ambrose!"

I gather Lane close and fuck her deeper. "I'm here."

I'll always be here. Lane Rhodes is *mine*, and I'm hers. The planets are back in alignment.

When the tremors start in her body, radiating out from her core, I send up a prayer of thanks to the mysteries of the universe. When Lane clamps down on me and comes for real, her head tossed back on the pillows and my thumb on her clit, I grit my teeth and hold on just long enough to feel her relax again, breathing hard.

Sweat slides down my back, and the room spins.

"Should I—"

"No." Lane's words are fuzzy, thick, but her eyes are clear when they meet mine. "Keep going."

Christ alive.

Heart pounding, I wedge myself as deep as I can go—then, ears ringing, pleasure stabbing my belly like a knife… I fill my girl to the brim.

61

* * *

Five years later

Two academics living in one house was always a recipe for chaos. Lane and I regularly leave scientific journals on top of the refrigerator or lodged between sofa cushions, and we both prefer pondering the great scientific questions to figuring out a grocery list. But we make it work, and it's just as well, because three months ago, we added even more chaos to the mix.

"Morning," I say, kissing my wife on the forehead where she sits in our comfiest armchair, the baby nestled against her chest. Lane slipped out of bed while I was showering for work at the college, and now she's hushing our son as grumbles and mouths at her nipple.

Breakfast all round, then. "Are you hungry?"

Lane beams up at me like I'm her personal angel. "*Starving.*"

Well, that won't do. We've always tried to keep things equal in this household, what with both of us working in the Physics department at the college, and when I try to spoil Lane too much, she won't let me. But since she got pregnant, I'm getting away with more and more: loads of laundry done in the background, meals cooked, dishes washed.

Thank god. This woman just casually created *life*, damn it. The least I can do is take extra care of her and our son.

Ten minutes later, I set a plate with a bacon sandwich on the side table by Lane's elbow, along with a glass of orange juice.

"Yeeeees," my wife groans, before blowing a happy raspberry on our baby's head. "You always make them better than I do."

"Well, I could teach you."

We've always liked private lessons.

But Lane pretends to think about it, then reaches over to flick my hip. "No, I don't think so. I like it when *you* make them for me."

Works for me. Jesus Christ, does that work for me.

I twirl a lock of blonde hair around my knuckle.

II

Tongue Tied

Description

~<del>⟨∘⟩</del>~

I 'm on the college debate team. I'm *good* at talking.

But when the head gardener looks at me, I can barely make a squeak.

When I was little, I got teased for having a stutter. All the other kids chattered away, while I struggled to form simple words.

I worked hard, had help, and got over that, damn it. I moved on. But when the handsome gardener looks my way in his fogged-up greenhouse, I'm tongue tied all over again.

He's just so *tall*, and broad, and there's this steadiness to him. Like the earth could crack apart, and he'd still be standing firm. Rooted deep.

When his green eyes find mine, I can barely stammer hello.

But my fierce blush does the talking for me...

Eden

❧

One month ago

O The walk to the greenhouse is cold. All across campus, the wind howls and rattles the college windows. It's that time of year when winter grapples with spring, and either season could come up victorious for the next week: choppy steel-gray waves headbutt the shore in the distance, while new blossom buds cling to tree branches, shivering too hard to open yet.

The sunshine is pale and watery. Bundled up in all my winter layers, my breath mists against my scarf where it pillows my chin, and my fingers are toasty-warm inside gloves. My boots thud across campus, along the coast path, and up the stone steps to where the greenhouse glass dome perches on the cliff side.

By halfway up the stone steps, I'm sweating, tugging my scarf loose and carrying it instead. When I reach the top, the wind blows clean through my clothes and I'm frozen again, my sweat chilled against my skin.

Shading my eyes against the bright sunshine, I turn in a slow circle, taking in the view. Long grass ripples across the clifftop, combed by the wind, while out at sea the waves foam at the mouth. Sunlight glints on the water, and seabirds screech as they play on air currents high above, while the town of Kephart spreads down below, spooning the college campus.

It's all so small down there—like a model town. I moved here from my identi-kit suburb two years ago, and every day this small town makes my heart thump faster.

But no sight hitches my breath like the Kephart greenhouse. Looming above the town on the clifftop, its glass walls sparkle in the sunshine, and there's a whole miniature rainforest shadowed inside.

I'm early. Of course I am. *Two whole years,* I've waited for my placement in this greenhouse, and today is my first day. As a Botany major… this is it. The promised land.

Tugging my gloves off with my teeth, I stuff them in my jacket pockets as I wander to the entrance. The heavy glass door is closed, but when I tug on the handle it swings open with a sigh of hot air.

Inside, through heavy strips of dangling plastic, it's another planet. A stream trickles somewhere nearby, hidden for the moment by the tangle of foliage. Everything is bigger in here: the trees stretching up toward the clouds, visible through the glass ceiling; the waxy green leaves, some the size of small canoes; the flowers; the jewel-toned butterflies that flit from plant to plant. It's hot and humid, and birds chatter up in the canopy.

"Hello?" The door swings shut behind me. Shrugging my backpack off, I stuff it with my scarf while peering through the tropical plants. "Is anyone here?"

The door was open, but should I not have come in? This greenhouse is the college's masterpiece, after all, and they don't even let tourists in, even though selling tickets could make a fortune. It's all about the *science* here, science and conservation, and no one is allowed in the greenhouse without an invitation and a supervisor.

"H-hello?" I try again, wincing at the faint stammer. It's been a long time since I struggled to speak clearly as a kid, and my old speech impediment hardly ever comes back to haunt me. Only when I'm super stressed or excited—and right now, I'm both. "Can anyone h-hear me?"

After freaking *years* of speech therapy, here I am still tripping over my words—and normally that makes my chest clench tight, but this morning, I'll give myself some grace. This greenhouse is the reason I picked Kephart College, after all, and I've spent two whole years down on that campus, staring longingly up at this cliffside. Of course I'm jittery right now.

Leaves rustle a short way down a winding stone path, and for a crazy moment, I think of tigers and giant snakes: creatures that hide in the jungle then strike like lightning, snatching their prey...

But of course it's a human man who steps onto the path, dressed in faded jeans and a navy blue t-shirt with the Kephart College logo. His shoulder length bronze hair is half pulled back, and a short beard clings to his square jaw.

"Hey!" he calls, beaming at me. "Be right with you."

The man smacks his gloved hands against his hips, glancing around him for dropped tools. His arms are tanned and toned, and his chest is broad with muscle. When he leans over to grab a small pair of pruning shears, those jeans cling to his taut ass.

Oh, god.

Wetting my lips, I shake my head to dislodge the ringing sound in my ears. No luck.

Who *is* that guy?

Behind me, the door swings open again, and another student pushes through the heavy strips of hanging plastic. I blink over my shoulder in a daze, nodding as my fellow Botany major and debate club rival, Jeremiah, peels off his sheepskin jacket in the sudden heat. Jeremiah jerks his chin up at me in return, eyes sparking with challenge.

Here we go.

Let's be honest: neither Jeremiah nor I would pick the other as our greenhouse placement partner. We've had too many vicious debates, tearing each other's argument to shreds; our Biology grades have come close too many times. Our strained relationship is nothing but sore spots.

But this is the Kephart greenhouse. For some things, you put your rivalries aside.

"Hey," I say, throat still tight as Jeremiah comes to stand by my shoulder. He's gazing up at the vines trailing from tree branches, and he barely registers the demigod with the pruning shears. Is he blind? "Can you believe this is finally happening?"

No stammer this time, thank god. The last thing I need is for my debate club rival to sniff out my weakness.

"About time," Jeremiah agrees. Then, eyeing me: "Think we'll be graded on a curve for this placement?"

Ugh. Who cares?

How can he think about that stuff *now*, with birds of paradise flitting overhead and the scent of damp soil in our lungs, and that—that *man* watching us both curiously as he walks over?

The man tugs off his gloves and tucks them in the back

pocket of his jeans so he can shake both our hands. From a distance, he looked roughly our age, but up close, you can tell this guy's older. He's built stronger than the average student, with faint lines at the corners of his green eyes, and there's a steadiness about him that says whatever the world wants to throw in his direction, he's seen it all before.

When his hand closes around mine, his palm is callused and dry. Sweat trickles down my spine, and the ringing sound is back in my ears, only louder.

"Hey, you two." It's a nice voice. Low and melodic—the kind of voice you might hear reading you bedtime stories on an insomnia app. "I'm Kai Akana, the Head Gardener here. I'll be taking care of you for the next couple months. You must be Eden and Jeremiah?"

Jeremiah says something in response, but I just nod in a daze. The man—Kai—smiles at me kindly, his eyes crinkling at the corners. Mid thirties, maybe? Hard to be sure when this man is so sun-kissed, with a deep tan and caramel streaks in his hair. He looks like the sun licked him all over.

Lucky sun.

"So are you both excited for your placement?"

"Definitely," Jeremiah says at once, all cool confidence.

I open my mouth to agree, but no words come. Chest tightening, I settle for another nod.

Oh hell.

"Great," the Head Gardener says, looking at me strangely now. That's two direct questions I haven't answered. "I'll show you where to leave your things, and then I'll give you guys the tour."

As I trail after Jeremiah and the demigod through the leaves, my tongue is glued to the roof of my mouth.

Forget a stammer.
Why can't I say a single word?

Eden

❧

Present day

"And another thing," I say, flinging a damp swim towel in my laundry hamper. "It's like Jeremiah thinks we're on some reality show where we might get voted out of the greenhouse. He acts like he's so charming and funny, making Kai laugh all the time. And he asks all these elaborate questions about botany, like such a try-hard."

"Isn't he a botany major?" my roommate's boyfriend murmurs. She shushes him, digging an elbow into his ribs where they're sitting together on her bed, backs leaned against the wall. She's blonde and feminine; he's dark-haired and dour. They're a beautiful pair, and they're both trapped here, listening to me.

Poor Lane. Poor Ambrose. He knocked on our door twenty minutes ago, trying to collect her for a date, but instead they've both been sucked into my vortex of doom.

It's like—all the words I *can't* say around Kai, all the words that get stuck in my throat in the Head Gardener's presence, they don't disappear after a while. Oh, no. Instead they wait in line until I'm back in my dorm room with people who don't make me too nervous to speak, and then they explode out of me in an incoherent burst.

My roomie deserves a medal. Or at least to go on a date with her sexy older boyfriend when he calls.

Instead I'm mid-rant, cleaning as I go, my cheeks hot with embarrassment and my voice hoarse from all this word vomit.

"You can leave, by the way." Holding up my waste paper basket, I sweep a medley of crap off my desk. Used post-it notes, book receipts from the library, and clothing labels from recent comfort-buys that I cannot afford patter against the base. "I know this is boring as hell."

No one wants to hear someone else's drama. Not in a twenty minute spew, anyway, and especially not when they should be on a hot date with their ex-tutor.

"It's not boring," Lane says valiantly, though Ambrose is studiously silent. Sometime in the last few minutes, his hand crept onto her thigh, and now his fingers toy with the hem of her skirt. Lane's cheeks are pink, and she keeps squirming. "Jeremiah's an asshole."

"Yeah." Slamming the waste paper basket back down, I point at my roommate like she just made a genius observation. "He totally is. He's been such a douche at debate club all month, mocking me for being silent in the greenhouse."

"Debate club?" Ambrose murmurs. He sounds confused, and I don't blame him. Half of this rant has been about how unfair it is that I'm twenty two years old and can't freaking speak.

"Obviously she can talk," Lane whispers back, and Ambrose rolls his eyes.

"Yes, obviously. We have first-hand evidence of *that*."

"Shh!"

God, now they're bickering. The most solid, stupid-in-love people I know are side-eyeing each other, and that's my fault. I did that.

At least he's still playing with her skirt. At least Lane's nibbling her bottom lip and staring up at him, her eyes going all hooded and hazy, their argument forgotten.

Hmm. Should *I* leave? They look like they need the privacy.

But then who would I finish this rant with, voicing these backed-up words? Guess I could take a shower, lecturing the tiles.

"Are you graded on participation?" Ambrose asks, his brisk tone all business. Lane shivers like it's the sexiest thing she's ever heard, but I try to ignore that and focus on her boyfriend. "Will it hurt your grade if you never ask any questions?"

My mouth drops open. I freeze with one hand against our mirror, scrubbing away the mascara marks and old smudges with a t-shirt from my hamper. Stress-cleaning the day away. "Oh, shit. I hadn't even thought of that."

Ambrose shrugs, but in a conciliatory way. Like he's sorry to be the bearer of bad news.

"We don't know that it matters," Lane puts in quickly, crossing her legs on her twin bed. It's so funny to see the two of them jammed together on the narrow dorm mattress, all long limbs and creaking bed springs, though surely they must get busy there sometimes when I'm gone.

Ack. No.

Not gonna think about that.

"Why don't you ask Kai how you're graded?" she says. I press my lips together and stare. Lane winces and adds: "In an email."

...Huh.

It's hard to imagine Kai Akana tip-tapping away on some fiddly little laptop—not with those callused hands and blunt, squared knuckles, and the way he seems like some magical creature that lives full-time in the greenhouse. Like they grew him from the soil for some research project, and now he curls up in the canopy to sleep at night, perched on by birds.

But he works for the college. He wears Kephart College t-shirts to work, and he always parks a college-branded truck out in the scrubby greenhouse parking lot.

Surely the Head Gardener has an email address. Is Lane right? Could I write Kai an email and prove that I'm not completely stupid—just selectively mute? Would he believe me?

"What would I even say?"

Ambrose raises an eyebrow. He's right: I've done nothing but say things since he knocked on our door twenty-some minutes ago.

Flinging my makeshift cloth in their direction, I scrub my face and turn away. "Oh, go on your date already. It's fine. I'll figure it out."

Lane's already sliding on her shoes, but her voice is worried. "Are you sure? I really don't mind staying, Eden."

She would, too. Just like I'd do anything for my roomie in return. Some of the girls are tense as hell with the roommates they were allocated, but not Lane and I. We won the jackpot, and I'll never take her for granted.

"Sorry for making you late," I say into her hair, squeezing Lane into a hug as she heads for the door. She smells like coconut, and she's wearing a white t-shirt tucked into a floral wrap skirt. Lane's been hard at work calling on spring since mid-January, and her efforts are finally paying off. It's still light out, and pink blossoms wave on the tree branches outside our window.

"Anytime." Lane squeezes me back. "Save the email as a draft and I'll help you go over it later."

"You're the best."

They both say goodbye, already reaching for each other with greedy hands as they spill out of the door, on their way to dinner or drinks or a movie or whatever it is loved-up couples do in Kephart. I wouldn't personally know.

As soon as the door swings shut behind them, I'm left in silence and a half-cluttered dorm room. My pulse thuds in my wrists, and dance music floats down the hall from the bathrooms.

I can do this. I can write Kai Akana an email.

Sucking in a deep breath, I stomp to the desk and lever my laptop open.

* * *

From: eden.hopkins@kephart.edu
To: kai.akana@kephart.edu
Subject: Surprise!! Can string words together after all :)

~~Dear Mr Akana~~

~~To whom it may concern~~

~~Hello!!!~~

Hey Kai,

Thank you so much for the greenhouse placement so far. I know I haven't mentioned this out loud, but I've been excited about this for YEARS, and it's everything I dreamed it would be. So… thanks. For that.

I have a quick question about our grades. I know some classes require active participation—asking questions, raising our hands, etc. This is going to be hard for you to believe, but I usually DO participate like that, but I'm having… ~~a medical issue a hormonal breakdown~~ some issues with speaking up in the greenhouse. You might have noticed.

Are we graded for active participation in that way? Can I send you questions via email instead? Would that work?? I know it's a lot to ask, and it would be extra effort for you, but I seriously cannot get a word out in that greenhouse. Please don't ask me why.

Okay, hope you have a great weekend. ~~I'm not insane, I promise.~~

Best,
  Eden

Kai

❧❧❧

H ere I've been, thinking my sweet undergrad is so scared of me that she can't say a peep. It's been messing with my brain, honestly. Whenever I'm walking through town late in the evening, I've been zigzagging back and forth across the road like some messed up chicken, trying to reassure the lone female walkers that I'm not following them.

I've been second guessing my beard, my clothes, my forearm tat. Even watched a true crime documentary one night, trying to compare my own looks to the perp's gaunt, dead-eyed stare.

Couldn't figure out why I give Eden the heebie jeebies so badly. I'm still not sure why, to be honest—but at least she's emailed me. That's something.

Hey Kai.

That greeting doesn't sound like someone who low-key thinks I'm a creep. At least, I'd like to think it doesn't.

Hope you have a great weekend.

Would she wish Ted Bundy a great weekend? Unlikely.

Leaning back in my kitchen chair, I scan Eden's email a second time, lingering for way too long on her email address. It's not like she's giving me her number—I know that. But now I have a way to contact her, don't I? Theoretically.

You know, if Eden ever felt like saying a single word in my presence. If she didn't go as pale as a ghost whenever I'm near, then flush bright pink when I look her in the eyes. If she weren't such a jittery little thing, her long, dark ponytail practically quivering whenever I brush by.

Jeez. Who am I kidding? I can never email this girl—not without good reason. With that in mind, I keep my reply short and blunt.

From: kai.akana@kephart.edu
  To: eden.hopkins@kephart.edu
  Subject: Re: Surprise!! Can string words together after all :)

Hey Eden,

Works for me.

Kind regards,
  Kai Akana
  Head Gardener

The email makes a little whooshing noise as it sends. I bury my face in my hands, my groan echoing around the kitchen. Thank god I live alone, because no one else needs to witness this low moment.

I hate knowing a young woman might be scared of me. Feels all sickly and wrong. And the worst part is—I *do* look at Eden more often than I should. I do make excuses to walk by her in the greenhouse, checking on her work in the plant beds; I do forget to blink sometimes when I stare at her. Pretty sure she caught me sniffing her shampoo once, too, when I stood behind her in the greenhouse. Mint and tea tree. So pretty and fresh.

But all that damning evidence aside, Eden's email hinted at a different problem. So… maybe I don't freak her out after all.

My chair judders back over the kitchen tiles as I stand, and I start to bang around my kitchen cupboards, fixing dinner. Oil heats in a wok, and I chop veggies blindly, lucky I don't lose a damn finger as my thoughts race.

Maybe it's the other undergrad—Jeremiah. There's a weird tension between those two. I sniffed it out in our very first session, noting the way they eyed each other warily; the way they danced around each other on the narrow paths. Truth be told, I thought maybe they liked each other—and god help me, did that jealousy eat me alive as I went home that day. But since then, I've figured they're way too frosty with each other to be crushing.

So maybe *I'm* not the one scaring Eden into silence.

Maybe Jeremiah's freaking her out.

Oh hell no.

As I slice up a red pepper, my chest puffs out and my grip tightens reflexively on the knife. The protectiveness rises up in me like a tsunami, unexpected but so powerful, urging me to do whatever it takes to make Eden Hopkins feel safe. Whatever. It. Takes.

Down, boy. Clearing my throat, I force my fingers to stop white-knuckling the knife handle and chop neatly. Better save those thoughts for when I'm not holding a deadly weapon.

Yeah.

* * *

Their next session is on Monday morning, and I watch that pair like a hawk. They both turn up early, like always—Jeremiah catching my eye, wanting to make sure I've seen him arrive, while Eden scuttles in behind him, her chin ducked. They walk together to the lockers tucked away by the glass wall, and when Jeremiah waves an arm, gesturing for Eden to go first, she nods and hurries ahead on the narrow path.

Is she running from him? Running scared?

Has he ever said something to her? Threatened her?

My hands ball into fists in my gloves, the dusty leather creaking, but I force myself to stay back and watch, ducked beneath a mossy branch. It's no good me tossing Jeremiah into the stream all 'cause Eden's twitchy in the greenhouse. Not without evidence that the reason is *him*. That's mob justice.

"Come on," I mutter, my words swallowed up by the babbling stream and flurry of wings. "Come on, Eden. Show me what's wrong."

I'll fix it, baby.

Outside, the sun rises over the cliff side, spearing shafts of golden light through the fogged-up greenhouse walls.

Their boots crunch on the stone path. They're walking back, stripped down to faded old t-shirts and torn jeans—no use wearing fancy clothes to garden. Everyone learns that lesson on day one. My students are both dark haired, skinny and pale, like in another world they could be siblings, and they're both tugging on raggedy gloves.

As I watch, my mouth so dry despite the damp air, Eden

turns her head and says something to Jeremiah. She *speaks* to him.

Ah, shit.

Eden will speak to that puffed-up, arrogant little undergrad, with his patchy attempts at facial hair and loud opinions on what makes a *proper* coffee? She'll chat to the guy who rolls his eyes when she takes too long to dig up a root, and who always leaves her to clean up the trowels?

So Jeremiah is not the problem. He's not the one freaking Eden out.

It *is* me.

"Damn." My curse is low and quiet, and I clear my throat before pushing the trailing vines aside and stepping out onto the path. Sure enough, Jeremiah smiles and tips his chin up in that universal bro greeting, while Eden flushes bright pink and jerks back a step, like she needs to huddle for protection behind Jeremiah.

As if that skinny little undergrad could save her from *me*. What would he do, debate me to death? Jeez.

I'm in a bad, bad mood. Never been a Monday-hater before, but here I am already craving the weekend and the feel of my board beneath me, rocking back and forth with the waves. Easing these troubles away.

"Morning, you two." Better to act like nothing's wrong, right? What else can I do? I've got skills to teach here. "We're looking at a diseased plant today. Gonna see if either of you can figure out the disease, and brainstorm ways to treat it."

"Like House," Jeremiah says, trailing after me down the winding stone path. Near our feet, something scurries back under cover of the foliage. A critter or a tiny bird, camouflaged to blend in with the dirt.

"Exactly like House." Sweeping a vine out of the way with my forearm, I wave them both off-path into the tangle. "And I'm the cranky asshole with the limp."

"You don't have a limp." Jeremiah's voice carries back through the leaves, always so confident. When I follow them both, the temperature drops a little in the shade.

"And you're n-not an asshole," Eden murmurs, so quiet I nearly miss it.

Their boots scuff away, and I stand frozen for three whole heartbeats. *Ba-dump. Ba-dump. Ba-dump.*

Did she—?

Was that—?

Am I hearing things now? Has talking to plants more than people finally taken its toll?

"Kai," Jeremiah calls. "Which plant is it?"

Right. Yeah. I've got a job to do—never mind the pretty undergrad frazzling my nerves.

The sickly orchid is in the under-story, tucked away from any bright rays of sunshine. We all squat around it, squinting at the splotchy leaves in the gloom.

"Mealy bugs," Jeremiah guesses.

"No."

"Rhizoctonia."

"No. Eden?" I turn my head, my voice gentling. "Want to guess?"

She inhales sharply, pressing her lips together. And god, the way she looks at me—the way her eyes widen, beseeching, like she wants me to understand—it wrecks me.

Eden's eyes are the same shade of gray as a hazy morning out at sea, bobbing on my surfboard in the mist. One of those days where the ocean and the sky blurs together, all pale, shifting light, and swimming feels one breath away from flying.

She jerks her head back and forth, ponytail swishing.

I sigh.

"Look here." On either side of me, they both lean closer, obediently looking at where I point. The orchid's stem has turned black near the soil, the stain disappearing into the leaf litter, and oily dark splotches have spread across its leaves. "See those lesions? They're like bruises. Now, what type of plant is this? Don't worry about specifics. Which family?"

"An orchid," Jeremiah says immediately, though Eden's lips move silently too. She knows, she just won't—or can't—say.

"And what causes those lesions in orchids?"

Jeremiah rocks back on his heels, nearly toppling back into the undergrowth. He doesn't care—he's solved the riddle. "Black rot!"

"Correct."

Beside me, Eden is silent, chewing on her lip. My knees ache from crouching for so long.

"There's might be a drainage issue around the roots. First, though, we're going to dig the plant up and check its neighbors. The last thing we need is fungus spreading through the greenhouse orchids, right?"

Two heads bob along in agreement. Jeremiah's chattering away—listing every factoid he knows about orchids and black rot—while Eden shifts forwards onto her knees, prodding gently at the soil with a trowel. This is standard for these two: Jeremiah does the talking, acting like a TV presenter on some nature documentary, while Eden quietly does the actual work.

"Wait a second, Eden."

She pauses, looking at me with those big, mist-gray eyes.

"Jeremiah can dig this one up. He needs to demonstrate more

practical skills."

There's a long-suffering sniff from my other side, then Jeremiah crashes forward onto his knees. He's a lot less graceful than his classmate. "Right, yeah. This will be a lot quicker if I do it. Move over, Eden."

She sits back on her heels, dabs at her forehead with her wrist, and offers me a shy smile. My other student grunts and mutters as he works, but I don't even glance over. I'm too locked-on to Eden, too busy staring and wondering and wishing I understood; wishing I knew if she's scared of me and why.

But Eden reaches over and brushes a piece of twig off my shoulder.

My heart lurches. *Not scared.*

"Little plant jackass," Jeremiah mutters, jamming the trowel into the soil.

Eden

～◦⊱✦⊰◦～

From: eden.hopkins@kephart.edu
To: kai.akana@kephart.edu
Subject: Sickly trees conundrum

From: eden.hopkins@kephart.edu
To: kai.akana@kephart.edu
Subject: Sickly trees conundrum

Hey Kai,

I was thinking about that orchid we dug up this morning, and what you said about the risk of fungus spreading. What do you do when the sick plants are the big trees? The ones holding up the whole canopy? You obviously can't move them, so... what then?

Best,
 Eden

PS. Thanks for making Jeremiah dig this one up. I tried teasing him about breaking a nail the other day, but he wouldn't take the hint. He had to get his hands dirty eventually, right?

* * *

From: kai.akana@kephart.edu
  To: eden.hopkins@kephart.edu
  Subject: Re: Sickly trees conundrum

Hey Eden,

Great question. There are things we can do to counter disease in the bigger trees—treatments and medicines; fungicides and selective pruning, etc. I'll show you my top tips next time you're in. But honestly, when it comes to the big boys... I do a lot of crossing my fingers and hoping they stay happy in the first place.

Kind Regards,
  Kai Akana
  Head Gardener

PS. You're welcome. Now we just need to get you chatting my ear off like Jeremiah...

* * *

From: eden.hopkins@kephart.edu
  To: kai.akana@kephart.edu
  Subject: Re: Re: Sickly trees conundrum

Hey Kai,

Don't hold your breath. Believe me, I would LOVE to bore you about orchids, but… it's not gonna happen.

Eden

* * *

"How about this: *Wanted: one conversation coach. Can you help me speak to the guy I like? Then call this number. Serious inquiries only, please.*"

There's a long, awkward pause in our dorm room. Ambrose rolls up one shirtsleeve, pointedly refusing to comment, while Lane sits beside him on her bed, wincing.

"I just think…"

My roomie fiddles with a bright pink highlighter in her lap, clicking the lid on and off. On and off. She's fidgety.

"I just think… an ad like that…"

"What's wrong with it?" Gathering my legs onto my desk chair and propping my chin on my knees, I squint at my laptop screen. My half-written ad barely fills two lines. How bad can it be?

"There's nothing *wrong* with it exactly," Lane says, click-clacking the highlighter lid. Click-clack. Her boyfriend reaches over without looking and plucks it from her hands, so Lane huffs and knits her fingers together. "I just think putting your number on an ad like that will get you a lot of weird voicemails."

"Agreed," Ambrose says. As always, his deep, clipped voice brings an air of gravitas, and I find myself deflating, reading my ad again.

"Shit," I say after the third read. "They'll think it's about dirty talk, won't they?"

Lane nods.

"Or they'll make it about that," Ambrose says.

Ew. "This is pointless."

"No!" Lane swats her boyfriend's shoulder, and he widens his eyes at her, as though to say: *What the hell do you want* me *to do about this?* "No, of course it's not pointless, babe. But maybe... maybe the only person you can really practice with is Kai. You know?"

For one brief, horrible moment, I imagine sending this ad to the Head Gardener. My stomach twists, and suddenly tonight's cafeteria pizza isn't sitting well.

"It worked for you two." Surly muttering doesn't look good on me, but I'm too bitter right now to care. "With your kissing lessons. This isn't even that! This is conversation lessons. Literally just: How to be a Human 101."

Footsteps thunder past our closed door and pound away down the hall, as shrieks of laughter seep through the walls. Dance music blasts from the bathrooms. At least someone out there is living the college dream.

"What about Jeremiah?" Lane tilts her head. "You speak to him with no problems, right? Maybe he could help you talk to guys?"

Ugh. "I just threw up in my mouth."

"Oh, stop it." Lane scrambles off the bed, and the mattress groans as Ambrose follows. "See, this is silly. You don't want to talk to just *some guy* as practice, you want to talk to Kai! So maybe you should do that. Make sure the environmental factors are all perfect, like with your orchid thingies, and then just... chat to him." My roomie shrugs into the jacket her boyfriend holds up, winking at me as she turns. "Take note cards with prompts on them if you need to. But do it, Eden. Start flexing that muscle. It's the best way, I promise."

"Have fun," I call as they both disappear through the doorway. Then, quieter: "Be grateful for each other."

Because I'd give anything to go to dinner like a normal girl with Kai Akana.

* * *

For the first time ever, I get to the greenhouse the next morning before Kai. I had this grand plan to get him alone; to spend at least ten minutes trying to chat with those mesmerizing green eyes before Jeremiah clatters in and throws me off. But judging by the red sun hovering barely over the horizon, I'm too much of a keen bean.

The salt breeze ruffles my hair and swishes the long clifftop grass this way and that. Leaning my back against the locked greenhouse door, I stare out to sea and let my mind go blissfully blank.

No fretting about essay due dates or obsessing over the email Kai sent me last night. No picturing the way his eyes crinkle when he smiles at me, or trying to summon his soil-and-citrus scent by memory.

Nothing but watching the pink-tinged sunshine sparkle on the waves.

My body aches beneath my worn jeans and faded red t-shirt, the chest blazoned with a band name I don't listen to anymore. Every time I shift, my tired muscles cry out, complaining about how these last few weeks have been way more exercise than I'm used to.

Still, it's a good feeling. Like my body's waking up after a long, deep sleep. I'm more aware of muscles I'd forgotten; when I need to sip water; and that tightness in my hips which means I need to go for a walk. And that's just from all the digging and pruning, never mind the parts of me which *Kai* has woken up—

"Eden!" His low, melodic voice floats on the morning air, as the Kephart College truck rumbles up a dirt track. He's got the driver's window wound all the way down, his tanned elbow leaning out, and Kai beams like he's honestly thrilled to see me this early.

It's nuts. At the very least, this man should be kind of tired of my nonsense—not parking haphazardly in the greenhouse lot then leaping out and jogging to my side.

"Excited to get going, huh?"

I start to nod automatically—then stop myself. Take a deep breath.

"Y-yes."

The word is ghostly quiet, almost as faint as the distant crash of waves, but Kai throws back his head and laughs like it's the best thing he's ever heard.

"There she is. Alright, Eden! Oh, this is gonna be a good day, I can feel it."

Shuffling out of his way, I watch the muscles flex in Kai's arm as he unlocks the greenhouse door and shoves it open. He's in his standard uniform of a navy Kephart College t-shirt, battered old jeans, and dusty hiking boots, and honestly, I don't understand why men would ever, ever wear anything else. He looks so freaking good, especially with the morning sunshine glinting in the caramel streaks of his hair, half tied back like usual.

Those aren't dyed highlights. Those are what happens when

a man spends hours and hours outside, tanning and moving his perfect body—and jeez, I need to put my tongue away. Does Kai hike? Rock climb? Surf?

I'm betting surf.

"D-did you s-sleep well?"

Kai's as patient as a saint as I force the question out, tripping over my words and practically chewing off my own tongue with frustration. He smiles gently as I duck under his arm, pushing my way through the hanging strips of plastic.

Just like always, the heat hits me like a damp cloth. This smell of soil and wet moss is my favorite smell in the whole world—except maybe Kai's citrus scent.

"Nope," the gardener says cheerfully, following me inside. The door whooshes shut behind him. "Tossed and turned all night, so much I barely slept a wink. But that was yesterday, am I right? And today is a brand new day, sweetheart."

Sweetheart.

I blink at the pet name, inwardly thrilled—and honestly, even though he said it, Kai seems as taken off guard as I feel. He clears his throat, a flush creeping over his cheeks, and nods at the lockers. "Go on and sort yourself out, then we'll get started. Jeremiah can join when he gets here."

But I don't want to start work yet.

Don't want to walk away to those lockers.

I want to push my luck and say another whole sentence to Kai, and maybe, just maybe, hear that pet name again.

"I–it's a st–stammer," I say, sounding out each word like I haven't had to do since I was a kid in speech therapy. "I'm not n-normally like this."

Kai's face falls. "Just with me?" he says, bracing like he's dreading the answer.

Already exhausted, I shrug.

"Shit." The Head Gardener curses quietly, but with feeling. He scratches his jaw, his short beard rasping. "That's what I was afraid of. Well, if there's anything I can do to make you more comfortable, Eden... any less scared..."

Scared?

Wait. What?

But Kai's backing up, palms raised like he's trying to soothe a skittish deer. Like he thinks I don't want him too near to me—and oh god, that's the worst joke I've ever heard. That is the exact opposite of what I want. I'd curl up and live in this man's armpit if I could.

Shaking my head, I step forward and grab Kai's raised wrist. His skin is warm and soft and alive under my palm, and his wrist is so thick, my fingers wrap all the way around but don't meet.

His eyebrows shoot up.

"Not s-scared," I say.

Nervous? Sure. Excited? Around Kai? All the time.

But *scared*? Never.

Kai swallows, his throat bobbing. We're so close now, I can make out brown flecks in those vivid green eyes. I can feel his body heat against my front, even in this humid greenhouse, and feel his pulse tip-tapping in his wrist against my fingertip.

"Tell me how to help," Kai says at last, his voice so low, and I don't even realize I'm swaying toward him until I nearly lose my balance and topple forward. When I catch myself against his strong chest, Kai flattens a sturdy palm over my hand, tugging me closer.

"Tell me," he says again.

I shrug, wishing like hell there was an easy answer. Like:

push this magic button, and I'll talk to you like a normal girl! If only.

My smile is heartbroken.

Kai smiles back, world-weary and so sad.

And his lips part like he's going to say something—but behind us, the door creaks open, and we both leap apart as Jeremiah calls, "Hello? Anyone here yet?"

Freaking early birds. Why couldn't Jeremiah sleep in, just this once?

Kai

꧁⚜꧂

When I was a kid, I was terrified of the ocean. All those critters under the surface, watching clueless swimmers with their googly eyes; all those riptides and whirlpools and freaky still patches; all those jellyfish stingers and shark's teeth. Get in there? Willingly? I wasn't crazy! I point blank refused to even learn to swim until I was nine years old, when my old man had enough of my bullshit and tossed me in the deep end of a neighbor's pool.

I thrashed and fought and choked down chlorine-flavored water. I didn't just make a meal of it—I served up a whole damn feast, fighting like a pool-sized kraken was trying to drag me under.

But my father watched from the pool's edge, arms crossed and face patient. And after a while, once it became clear that he wasn't buying my drowning act, I stopped fighting the water and just… floated. Heart pounding but my narrow kid's body so light.

"There you go," my dad rasped, his voice ruined by smoke

and by singing along with the radio at top volume as he drove supply trucks across the country. He crossed to a sun lounger and tugged a paperback out of his back pocket before sitting down. "Get practicing, 'cause we're going in the sea on Saturday."

And that was that.

I'd be lying if I said that I never get the shivers out on the ocean anymore, even as a grown man. Sometimes, when a tendril of seaweed brushes my leg or something spooks the seagulls further out, sending them squawking up into the sky, my heart thumps so fast it feels like it might burst.

But I still get my butt in that ocean every morning before work. I still spend hours on my board each weekend, drifting and bobbing, and when the waves are good, I soar like a goddamn eagle. Nothing else makes me feel so alive... except maybe Eden's fingers wrapped around my wrist.

You can live with fear—that's all I'm saying. You can learn to sit with it.

Nerves can become old friends.

"Ever heard of immersion therapy?"

Eden's running through the standard weekly checks in the greenhouse, strolling from plant to plant with a clipboard and stubby pencil. It's a basic sweep to check for obvious signs of disease and predation—for anything I might need to troubleshoot, basically. It's a vital task, but after watching her work for several weeks, I trust Eden to do it.

She glances over at me, frowning as she smiles. "N-no. What's that?"

This girl has said more to me over the last few days than in the whole month before that. She's getting quicker, too, smoothing her way through simple sentences, and she stammers less—not that I'm gonna point it out.

"It's when people treat phobias by kinda throwing you in the middle of 'em. So say you were scared of spiders—"

"N-not a lie." Eden ticks off a box on the checklist, grinning at me as she steps off-path into a small grove of banana trees. The fruits hang in clumps, like fistfuls of curved green fingers. Not ripe yet.

"Right. Yeah, exactly." What was I saying? It's so hard to focus when Eden lets me close to her side, with her long, dark ponytail swishing between her shoulder blades. There's that whiff of mint and tea tree shampoo again. "So you're afraid of spiders, and then to treat you, they put you in a giant spider tank."

"Oh my *god*." Eden shudders, clutching the clipboard tight before turning back to her list. "I'd r-rather stay scared."

That's fair. Not my best example, maybe.

"Well, or say you were scared of something less freaky. Like kittens or chocolate buttons. Or, I dunno... a certain gardener..."

Eden's soft laugh is the best sound I've ever heard. She peers up at each of the banana trees, examining them closely before checking them off the list. "Are you going to throw me in a K-Kai Akana tank? I told you before, I'm n-not scared."

And those are the sweetest words to my ears. Still: "You *are* nervous around me, though."

Eden shrugs, blushing prettily as she steps past me back onto the path. I follow, reluctant to get back on the path where Jeremiah can see us from where he's crouching by the stream collecting samples.

Not that Eden and I are doing anything worth looking at. But still.

I like the illusion of privacy.

"So maybe if we spend more time together, you'll be less nervous around me."

Eden nibbles on her bottom lip, and she won't meet my eye as she wanders down the stone path, then steps off again to inspect an açaí palm. I follow, throat tight.

"I don't think that w-will help," she says at last, and my heart sinks before she adds: "We could try, though."

My heart floats back up again like a helium balloon. And— the tips of Eden's ears have turned pink. Huh. That's interesting.

But... why won't it help?

And why exactly is this girl nervous around me, anyway?

Are they... you know. The *good* kind of nerves?

"Eden," I say slowly, checking over my shoulder to make sure there's no sign of Jeremiah. The path is empty behind us and we're surrounded on all sides by thick, tangled foliage. Overhead, trees loom and vines dangle and birds flit from branch to branch as sunshine sparkles through fogged glass. It's like we're in our own private universe. "Are you up for a quick experiment?"

She hums, idly checking off another box with the stubby pencil.

I stroll around to face her head on, waiting until she glances up at me to smile. Those mist-gray eyes widen.

"Does this make you nervous?" I say, my own heart thumping against my ribs. "When I look at you?"

Eden shrugs, but her cheeks are bright pink.

"Well, what about when I talk to you? Is that it?"

She's not the only one with a belly full of snakes right now if so—and I sound hoarse, like the words are scraping my throat on their way out. Eden inhales sharply and shakes her head. Her grip is tight on the clipboard.

"How about now?" My boots thud against the dirt as I step forward once… twice… moving slowly so Eden can back away if she needs. But my sweet, shy undergrad raises her chin and waits for me to get closer, visibly nervous but defiant.

I *know* that glint in her eyes—it's like me heading out on the waves each morning on my board. It says: *screw you, brain. Some things are worth fighting for.*

"Eden," I say softly, navy t-shirt sticking to my damp back. The air is so hot and thick in this greenhouse, and the stream sloshes nearby over mossy pebbles. "Can I touch you?"

Probably shouldn't. She's a student, after all, and though I'm no lecturer, I bet if I flicked through the employee handbook gathering dust in a drawer at home, I'd find a section warning me away from this.

But I don't care. A job is just a job, you know?

This is Eden. This is more important.

She darts a glance over my shoulder, checking the path behind me for signs of her classmate. And when she looks back at me and gives that tiny nod… man alive, I could crash to my knees.

"Okay," I say instead, like this is a totally normal conversation. A completely reasonable experiment for me to run. "Does *this* make you nervous?"

My palm settles on her shoulder, holding lightly to her slender body. Barely touching her at all, especially when you take the thin layer of her t-shirt into consideration.

But Eden's pulse taps at the base of her jaw, fast and urgent, and I can *see* it, can feel it thrumming beneath my fingertips, and holy shit, this is happening. I've been dreaming about this girl for weeks, and now she's solid beneath my hand.

"N-no," Eden whispers.

"How about this?" My palm moves to cup the side of her neck, thumb brushing against that frantic pulse point. When Eden swallows, her throat shifts against my hand, and fuck, I want to touch her everywhere. Every inch.

"No," she whispers, glancing over my shoulder again. "K-keep going."

"Here?"

A single fingertip trails down her upper arm.

Eden shakes her head, blowing out a breath.

"And this?"

I pluck one hand away from the clipboard and knot our fingers together—and it feels so *right*. Eden grips back like she needs this too, like we're both clinging to a lifeline, and god, I don't know what I'm doing here. All I know is I never want to stop.

"N-no," she says.

But that stammer is still there, and she's still tensed up and fidgety. Eden gazes up at me like I hung the goddamn moon—but she *is* nervous, no matter what she says.

"Liar." Ignoring the good sense howling in the back of my brain, I raise our joined hands and brush a kiss against Eden's knuckles. Her hands are chapped and raw, and I make a mental note to bring her hand cream tomorrow. "Don't be scared of me, sweetheart."

Though I hate breaking contact, I let go of her hand and step back.

And just in time—Jeremiah clatters around the corner and stomps off the path, moving with as much stealth as a cranky elephant, despite his gangly frame. He shows me a sample, frowning at the slick of algae on a lollipop stick. "Is this going to be a problem?"

I sure hope not.

* * *

From: eden.hopkins@kephart.edu
  To: kai.akana@kephart.edu
  Subject: Our experiment earlier

Sometimes nerves are a good thing. Just saying.

Eden

* * *

From: kai.akana@kephart.edu
  To: eden.hopkins@kephart.edu
  Subject: Re: Our experiment earlier

Tell that to my blood pressure. ;)

Kai

Eden

꧁꧂

Sometimes, when my thoughts are loud and buzzy and my body is restless and it feels like I'll never, ever fall asleep again, I go wandering around campus late in the evening. There's something soothing about seeing the lights on in the library windows, and knowing that people are studying for exams and writing essays and stress-eating snacks from vending machines, all of them also too wired to think about sleep right now.

Or hearing the party-goers stagger back from town, whooping and laughing and chasing each other around the quad, and feeling the knowledge deep in my bones that everyone has their own vivid story to tell.

I like seeing dog walkers from town cut across campus to get to the coast path, their furry friends stopping to sniff every lamppost and bench. I like the way the dogs and drunk people lose their minds together, each so excited to bump into the other.

I like the fogged windows of the Brainy Bean, open 'til late, and the college girls wearing their boyfriends' hoodies, the pouches stuffed full of snacks for movie night.

I like the moonlight glinting out on the water in the distance, and the speckled stars in the night sky. And I like the silhouette of the greenhouse, looming high on the clifftop above campus. A constant reminder of what happened earlier.

Where does Kai live in town? What is he doing right now? Does he ever think of me when he's not at work?

Kai, Kai, Kai.

I'm a stuck record, and I don't even care. He's all I want to think about, replaying our stolen moments together over and over like a favorite home movie in my brain.

The way he spoke to me earlier, his low voice hushed, green eyes burning bright. The way he touched my shoulder, my neck, my upper arm—the way he took my hand and kissed it. *Kissed* it. Holy hell.

And yeah, I know that kiss was as chaste as it gets, his lips barely brushing my knuckles, but... wow. My core temperature has been raised ever since.

As I power walk around campus, I'm cooking under my clothes, hot and restless and achy between my legs. Needing *more.* More touch, more words, more teasing smiles from Kai Akana. More secret experiments, tucked away together in the miniature rainforest on the hill.

More chances to prove that I *can* speak, I can talk to this man, damn it.

I could be with him... if he wanted me.

Does he want me?

For the first time, it doesn't seem impossible.

My feet carry me along the campus paths, weaving a nonsensical trail, and I catch snippets of conversation as I stride past open windows. People are gossiping about parties, studying for tests, arguing about whose turn it is to take all the stolen mugs back to the cafeteria. Living their lives.

On the north side of campus, the auditorium doors are thrown open wide, a shaft of warm light spilling over the paving stones outside. Voices carry out into the darkness, projected in that special way that actors have, and I pause in the shadows, peering through the doorway.

The stage is bare, the set not yet built, and a young man and woman stand opposite each other under a spotlight, each declaring fervent love for the other. The man cups the young woman's cheek, and she melts closer to him, saying how much she longs for him.

My heart pangs.

"Good, aren't they?"

The quiet voice makes me jump, and I let out a yelp before seeing Sylvie, a girl from my dorm, leaning against the auditorium brick wall in the shadows. She huffs a laugh, her whole body bundled up in a men's gray woolen sweater. Whose is *that*? It looks way too nice to belong to a student.

"Sorry, Eden" Sylvie says. "Didn't mean to make you jump. I'm waiting for my chance to rehearse."

Oh, right—Sylvie is a drama student. I remember being surprised about that before, shocked that a shy, quiet girl like her would ever want to stand on-stage in front of a crowd. But hey, what do I know? Being around Kai Akana scares the crap out of me, even calls my ancient stammer back, and I still want to do it for every minute of every day. So maybe I *do* understand.

"Which part are you playing?" The last English class I took is a distant memory, but even I know Romeo and Juliet when I see it.

"Understudy for Juliet." Sylvie's smile is bitter. "One of these days, I'll get an actual role. You know, when someone sees past all of *this*."

She gestures at her short, curvy body, swamped in the mystery sweater. For Sylvie's sake, I hope she's right. At least no one in Botany is gonna judge me for stuff like that.

"Hey, maybe Juliet will sprain her ankle." I nod at the young woman inside, clinging to Romeo's shirt like she wants to tear it clean off. "Not a break or anything serious." I wink in the gloom. "Just a sprain."

Sylvie snorts and scrubs both hands down her face. "I feel guilty even thinking about that."

"Are you ready?" An older man suddenly appears in the doorway, his gaze skating past me to settle on my dorm mate. He's handsome and stern, his dark eyebrows lowered, and Sylvie can't hide her shiver as she blinks up at him. Is that how I look at Kai?

"Yes." She pushes off the wall, fiddling with those too-long sleeves. "I'm ready. Bye, Eden."

"See you."

As they duck back inside, I finally point my feet toward the dorm, my thoughts whirling.

Sylvie is brave. Even though she's shy, even though people don't always see past her looks, she loves acting, and so she fights to get onstage.

Meanwhile, I've let my stammer hold me back with Kai. Even though I've wanted him from the beginning, even though I've crushed hard on him for weeks, I've held back and hidden, too scared of humiliation.

But maybe I can fight too.

Maybe it's time.

***

It's a rough night. The radiator is broken in our room, cranking to life at weird hours and spilling molten heat that cooks us in our beds. I toss and turn, kicking the sheets down my body and sweating through my pajamas, while across the room, Lane sleeps through it all, oblivious.

When I do finally fall into a fitful sleep, weird dreams play through my brain like a slideshow: wading into the sea next to campus and getting stuck, my legs trapped in wet cement; pulling out my teeth one by one and slotting them into a piggy bank on my desk; jumping off the tallest branches in the greenhouse and soaring through the canopy with the other birds.

In that last dream, I get tangled in a vine, trussed up and dangling there. I'm trapped, cheeping helplessly, until Kai rescues me, cupping my little bird body between his palms.

Yeesh.

Thanks, brain.

One cold shower, a plate of toast that tastes like cardboard, and approximately three dozen coffees later, I shove through the greenhouse door. Usually, I enjoy the rush of warm air, but today I'm still overheated and cranky, traumatized by my fever-dreams. I smack the dangling plastic strips out of the way, grumbling under my breath. Will I ever cool down?

"Oh ho ho," Kai calls, jogging down the path to meet me. *He* doesn't look like he slept horribly. His skin is tanned and clear, his green eyes are bright, and his chestnut hair has a healthy sheen where it's tied half back. White teeth flash as the gardener grins. "Morning, sunshine. You look ready to rip some heads off."

Poking my tongue out, I stomp past him to the lockers.

Kai's not wrong. But I'd never rip *his* head off.

Too pretty.

"Bad night?" He trails after me, and if he weren't talking, I might never know he was there. For a tall, muscled man in dusty hiking boots, Kai Akana is surprisingly light on his feet.

I grunt, shoving my backpack in an empty locker.

Two palms land on my shoulders, and I nearly jump out of my skin. But it's—this is real. The head gardener is rubbing my shoulders, his strong fingers kneading away the tension in my muscles. He's comforting me, smoothing away my bad mood just like that... and *god*, it feels good.

Gusting out a weak sigh, I sag back against his chest. Lips nuzzle my temple, his short beard tickling my skin. Oh, jeez.

"Do you need me to kick someone's butt? Is it Jeremiah?"

I snort, shaking my head, and my insides explode with light when Kai kisses me properly, planting an undeniable smooch right on my cheekbone.

"I'd do it, you know. I'd do it for you." His voice is low, raspy, and it sends tingles all the way to the base of my belly. My back rests against his toned chest, and I take all my grumping and grousing back—I *love* this heat. The warmth of Kai's body; his breath tickling my ear; the humid greenhouse air. All of it. Cook me alive, damn it.

"Eden." Kai squeezes my shoulders gently, and I turn to face him. I should step back, should put some distance between us, but I don't. This close, I can count the faint freckles on the bridge of his nose. "Tell me about it. Go on, I dare you."

Crap. Well, here goes. I said I'd be brave, didn't I?

"I d-didn't s-sleep well."

Ugh. *Why?* Why can I speak to literally anyone else on this campus with zero issues? Why does a single glimpse of this man glue my tongue to the roof of my mouth? So humiliating.

But Kai doesn't act like he's bored as he waits for me to sound the words out. He's patient, smiling kindly, still kneading at my shoulders—though now we're facing each other, it feels even more intimate.

Square on with Kai, I feel like Juliet from last night. Like I want to collapse against his chest, and tear his t-shirt clean in two, and declare to the world that he's my sun and moon, and if I can't have him, I'll burn down Verona.

Instead, I force a smile, though it feels more like a grimace. "I had these w-weird dreams."

A cocky grin. "Was I in them?"

Yes. Untangling my wings from a vine, then cupping me against his chest so he could feel my rapid, songbird heartbeat.

For obvious reasons, I will take that to my grave.

"Nope. Y-you wish, Akana."

Kai steps even closer, his gaze roaming over my features before resting on my mouth. His chest rises and falls beneath his navy t-shirt. "Yeah, I definitely do."

Oof. Now what?

I glance at the greenhouse door, but for once, there's no sign of Jeremiah. We're alone.

Damn. Okay.

I wet my lips, and Kai watches the pink flick of my tongue like it's the most fascinating thing in the world. He doesn't stop me, not as I place both palms on his chest, not as I push onto my toes, boots creaking, and not as our mouths come a breath apart.

"Eden. Baby." Kai's hands leave my shoulders and grip my waist instead, squeezing me through the thin fabric of my t-shirt. For years, I've been waiting for my womanly curves to arrive, but they seem to be lost in the mail—but Kai doesn't mind. He inhales sharply, tugging me so my front presses against his chest.

Our lips brush.

My head swims.

A bird shrieks overhead, flapping loudly from one branch to another. I know how it feels. If I could take off in an overloaded flurry of wings, maybe I would.

But I'm a boring old human, so instead I clutch at Kai's t-shirt and kiss him again—harder this time. He tilts his head down and kisses me back, patient and coaxing, never pushing, and all the while, his heart goes *thump, thump, thump* beneath my palm.

He's so sturdy and warm.

Does Kai like this too?

Are his insides all giddy and sparkly? Do men get like that? Because *I* feel like I'm ready to float up to the canopy, but maybe this is a boring, newbie kiss. Maybe it's dull. Panic twists in my chest, and I part my lips and slide our tongues together.

"Mm." Kai's low rumble of approval makes me shiver all over. This time, when he kisses me back, I sway back from the force of it, clinging to him for balance. He's strong and hungry, devouring my mouth, and our boots scrape against the stone path as we pant together, clawing to get closer—

"Hey," Jeremiah calls, the door swinging open. Kai and I leap apart, both flushed and wild-eyed, as my classmate shrugs past the plastic strips and turns for the lockers. He pauses when he sees us—both silent, both breathing hard—but Jeremiah doesn't call us out on it. He slips between us, one eyebrow raised.

"What's the plan?" Jeremiah's bag clangs into an empty locker, and he peers back at us both over his shoulder. We're both still frozen, our brains offline. A glove slips out of Jeremiah's back pocket and lands with a soft smack.

"Propagation," Kai says, a beat too late, while I crouch down and pick up the dropped glove, so pathetically grateful for something to do with my hands. My classmate grunts his thanks when I stand up and pass it to him, eyeing me curiously. "We're taking cuttings today."

If we can act normal for a few hours, anyway.

Seems unlikely.

Kai

ᘒᘒᘒ

By evening, Eden's kiss is still wreaking havoc on my body and brain. It's like the second her lips touched mine, a bunch of nerves frazzled under my skin, and my thoughts got snarled in an infinite loop.

Eden. Eden. Eden.

She's all I can think about. The feel of her warm, toned waist beneath her t-shirt; the way she sighed into my mouth and melted against my chest.

That mint and tea tree scent of her hair.

The teasing smile she gives me sometimes.

And the way she often trips over my name, but takes the trouble to say it anyway.

God knows how we made it through a whole session on propagation earlier, but we did. My mouth recited the lesson by heart—I'm lucky I've taught this all so many times before—but my insides went haywire every time I glanced at Eden.

Holy hell. That *kiss.*

My surfboard bobs over the waves, icy spray flecking my

face. Even though I'm zipped into a thick wet suit, the cold gnaws on my bones. It's early in the year to be in the water, and this is nothing like the warm sea back home where I learned to surf in nothing but board shorts.

Every time I get splashed, it's like hundreds of tiny needles pricking my skin. When I lick my lips, I taste salt.

The sky is gray, gray, gray.

Don't care. I *need* to be out here right now, feeling the ocean buoy my body. Chasing the high of a perfect wave. Need the distraction from my sweet undergrad and the press of her palms against my chest; need to calm down the jitters under my skin. It's an overcast evening and these conditions aren't great, but they're taking the edge off at least.

Wind gusts inland, ruffling the tops of the waves on its way and chilling me through my wet suit. The water's getting choppier, and the swell is rough. Gray clouds darken overhead.

Risky.

Still, I linger for a while longer, catching a few more waves—trying to burn off even ten percent of this nervous energy crowding my chest.

Eden.

Is she obsessing too? Would she kiss me again? The thought that she might not, that this might all be happening solely in my head, makes me want to slam my forehead against my surfboard.

How can I teach her for the rest of the semester, acting normal? How can I hide the *insanity* I feel for her, the irrepressible need to have her in my arms?

The swell comes out of nowhere, so fierce and fast that I'm nearly knocked off my board. I cling on, muscles straining and teeth gritted, until the world levels out again and I'm safe.

Overhead, seagulls ride the wind and cackle.

It's no use.

Pointing my board toward land, I cut through the water with powerful strokes.

Only one person can fix this.

* * *

From: kai.akana@kephart.edu
To: eden.hopkins@kephart.edu
Subject: SOS

Sweetheart,

I'm going insane. Meet me in the greenhouse if you see this tonight.

Yours,
Kai

* * *

From: eden.hopkins@kephart.edu
To: kai.akana@kephart.edu
Subject: Re: SOS

On my way.

Eden

* * *

Even though I know Eden is coming, I still pace around the greenhouse like a caged tiger. It's different in here at night— waist-high lamps light the paths, and with the sky ink-black outside, the greenhouse floor is reflected in the ceiling. When I run my hands through my hair, my reflection above does that too—except smaller and warped and upside down, half blocked by shadowy branches.

The birds are quiet and still, roosting in the canopy, and the vines seem to stretch longer where they dangle down, reaching toward the paths. The trees look bigger at night.

My boots scrape against the gritty stone path. Water burbles over rocks in the stream.

The air is thick and hot and humid, and when Eden pushes through the greenhouse door, it pools in my lungs like toffee sauce.

"You came." The words have barely scraped out of my throat when she runs to me, leaping into my arms. Eden is tall but so light, and I lift her easily, spinning us both around. High above, our reflections whirl like tops, clinging together.

Never want to put her down.

Never want to let go.

I do—but for the record, I hate it.

"I got your email," Eden says, her cheeks pink and her smile wide, and though I don't want to point it out and make her self-conscious, this is the first time she's spoken to me without stammering. Want to hoist her onto my shoulder like an Olympic champ. "Something about going insane?"

She laughs when I groan, tugging her close again. Fitting her hips against mine. Screw keeping a proper distance. Screw taking things slow.

I *need* this girl.

"That kiss," I tell her, placing her arms around my neck. Eden bites her lip and slides her fingers into my hair. "That goddamn kiss, Eden. I'm wrecked."

"M-me too."

Thank god.

It's so hard to concentrate when Eden's fingertips are scratching at my scalp. So hard to think of anything right now except tasting her again—everywhere. I swallow hard, fighting to keep on track.

"Listen. This isn't a one-time thing for me, sweetheart. I don't do flings with students. I don't do flings, period. So this is serious for me. Can you handle that?"

She hums, twining a lock of my hair around her finger.

"Eden," I say weakly. "Baby, I need the words."

She gazes up at me, misty eyes shining bright. "I c-can handle that. I want that too."

"You do?"

A slow nod.

My heartbeat is ragged. It's everything I wanted to hear, but now I'm struggling to believe her words. Has any man ever been so lucky? What have I ever done to deserve this?

Must have been a dung beetle or something in a previous life. Must be owed some serious karma.

A bird coos overhead, feathers rustling as it gets comfy on its branch. Eden's breath hitches when I duck down, running the tip of my nose along her cheekbone. Her skin is like satin.

"You're mine," I say, testing out the words.

"Y-yours," Eden agrees, and fuck, the wave of need that rises up in me—it's stronger than the swell that nearly knocked me sideways earlier. My knees buckle, and Eden comes with me as I stagger two steps to the left, cupping her cheeks and dragging her mouth to mine.

"Mmph!"

She kisses me back hungrily, scrabbling at my shoulders and tugging at my shirt. Don't even know what I'm wearing, and I tear away quickly to glance down. A plain white t-shirt, gone kinda grungy from years of washing, with the hem frayed where it meets my old jeans. Shit. Still, at least Eden doesn't seem to care one bit about my worn closet.

Just like I don't want her any less for her plaid pajama pants and baggy black sweater. If anything, seeing Eden so natural, so comfortable, so *raw,* makes me want to rip her clothes off even faster. I kiss her again, and she laughs against my mouth as I tease the hair-band from her dark hair, freeing that ponytail.

Soft hair spreads over her shoulders. A small hand creeps under my t-shirt, stroking up my bare stomach, and agonized need twists in my gut like a hook.

This time when I kiss her, my pulse thuds in my ears.

"What will we t-tell Jeremiah?"

Eden plucks my jeans button open, and I huff and squeeze her perfect ass. "Don't say another man's name right now. My control is hanging by a thread."

Eden laughs, the sweet sound echoing around the greenhouse. "Well, then maybe you should let go."

That's another sentence without stammering. Fierce pride glows in my chest, and I take Eden's wrist, tugging her down onto the dusty stone path.

"Sit on my lap. Yeah—like that."

Not gonna make my girl sit down in the dirt. Hell no.

That's *my* job here, and I am very fucking happy to do it. The stone is warm and flat, but I'd sit on a bed of nails if it meant getting closer to Eden.

Down here, we're level with the under-story: the flowers and ferns and other small plants that carpet the rainforest floor. The stream is louder, too.

"We'll tell Jeremiah that we're dating, but that we'll keep it out of the greenhouse. How's that?"

Eden presses her lips together, fighting a laugh, and pointedly looks all around.

"Yeah. Well." I grip her hips and squeeze, rocking our bodies together. "While he's here too, anyway. This is after hours in the greenhouse—doesn't count. And what Jeremiah doesn't know can't hurt him."

Besides, it's none of his business. It's none of *anyone's* business, and down here, cocooned by shadowy leaves, it'll stay that way.

Eden must agree, because she knits her fingers behind my neck and kisses me deeply, squirming in my lap like she's impatient for this too. God, I hope so. She's panting now, hot and flushed and so fucking sweet, and my heart pounds out a war beat against my ribs as she writhes in my lap.

"Do you feel what you do to me, Eden?" My voice is rough.

She nods and rocks against my length, riding the hard ridge of my cock through my jeans. It's the best kind of torture. Her eyes are hazy.

"C-can we...?"

My gut twists even tighter. "Hell yeah. If you want to, sweetheart."

Eden smiles, so shy even now, with her lips red-raw from kissing me. "I don't know what I'm doing. But I w-want to."

Thank god. I'm wound so tight, I might explode if I don't press inside my girl. Need to feel her wet heat; the tight grip of her strangling me; the scrape of her teeth against my neck.

Need to fuck that shyness away, and hearing that I'll be her first only makes my blood pump hotter. But first…

I lay back on the stone path and pat my chest.

"Take those pants off and come sit here."

Eden

⤛⤜

It's so surreal, standing up on wobbly legs and seeing Kai Akana stretched out on the stone path below me. His hair glints in the lamplight, and his white t-shirt strains over his muscled chest. When he catches me staring, he flashes a cocky grin.

"Up here." Kai pats his chest again, right on the sternum. And I know what he's offering—I've read romance novels, damn it—but that doesn't take the squirmy, embarrassed feeling out of my stomach. My thumbs hook over the waistband of my pajama pants but I pause, mind racing.

What if I'm *weird* down there?

What if I'm deformed and I don't even know it yet?

I mean, I showered and, you know, trimmed everything neatly, but what if I pull my underwear down and Kai flinches away?

This is the problem with saving yourself for someone special. It all sounds smart and romantic beforehand, but then you find yourself completely clueless when the stakes are highest.

"Eden." The head gardener looks less cocky now, his handsome face unsure. "We don't have to do this, sweetheart. We can just talk."

Kai moves to tip over, rolling to one side, and I block him with my calf. "No, wait! Sorry. I'm just n-nervous. I want to do this, I swear."

And I really, really do.

Besides, Lane went after the man she wanted, and now they're together and stupid in love. Sylvie puts herself out there again and again, chasing her dream of acting on stage.

I can do this. I can be brave.

I won't be the only friend who's a giant, cowardly chicken, damn it.

"P-promise you won't laugh?"

Kai looks so offended, *I* nearly burst out laughing.

"What kind of jackass do you think I am?" He settles back on the stone path, green gaze fixed on me, and taps his chest one more time. "Come on, sweetheart. Have a little faith."

Okay.

Yeah.

My pajama pants whisper down my legs, puddling around my ankles. Taking a deep breath, I hook my thumbs around my panties and slide those down too, then kick everything onto the rocks lining the path.

Kai is still and silent, a tendon corded in his neck. His gaze on me is hot enough to sear my skin.

"Beautiful," he rasps as I step awkwardly to either side of his neck, kneeling down and sitting back on his chest. "Everything about you is beautiful, Eden."

His short beard tickles my inner thigh. Kai turns his head and kisses me there, so sweet and intimate that my toes curl.

Then he nips, eyes wandering back to mine in challenge, and suddenly my blood is pounding through my veins once again.

Oh, it's on.

My low belly is heavy with need, pulse throbbing between my legs.

I'm slick and swollen. Achy and bared to Kai's hungry gaze.

After one last pause, I shrug my sweater off too, baring myself completely.

You're naked, a voice whispers in my brain as Kai slides two strong, callused hands beneath my ass and lifts me to his mouth. *You're naked in the greenhouse with the sexy head gardener. And you're about to sit on his face.*

So surreal.

"T-tell me if I squish you."

Kai winks at me, his breath hot against my bare slit. "Not possible, sweetheart."

Then he tugs me down and the world turns hot and wet and blurry, my pulse slamming in my ears as the head gardener licks and sucks me into oblivion, his groans vibrating against my clit.

Don't know where to put my hands, so I try Kai's forehead, the tops of my thighs, and his stomach, before pinching my own hardened nipples. Pleasure lances through me, and I shudder against Kai's tongue.

Oh, *shit.*

At some point, my head tips back, dizzy from pleasure. My reflection high above does the same, swaying above her own prone man. We're both flushed and rumpled and wild, and I barely recognize myself up there. Is that the girl who can barely get her words out in Kai Akana's presence? Is that *me*?

"Eden." Kai squeezes my ass in both hands, yanking me

impossibly closer, devouring me like a starving man. "Eden. So fucking sweet. Christ, I could do this forever."

But—no, he couldn't. Not when the scrape of his teeth over my clit makes me flush red-hot all over, and not when his tongue pushing inside me makes me wail. My knees give out before the rest of me, tremors wracking my whole body, and thank god Kai can hold my whole weight, else he'd be smothered alive.

Green eyes watch me as I come, not blinking even once. His tongue strokes me through it all, delving between my folds.

When I finally collapse backward, tumbling onto his chest, Kai grins at me. His short beard is slick.

"There she is. Had enough for one night?"

Oh, hell no.

My fingers are clumsy when I reach back, but somehow I get his jeans all the way open and draw his cock into the humid air. It's long and thick, the skin tan against my pale hand, and so hard it must surely be painful.

Kai hisses between his teeth as I stroke him twice, my arm twisted awkwardly behind my back, his hips bucking up into my touch. And it's powerful to be above him like this, to draw these ragged groans from Kai, but the angle is all wrong. I let go to crawl back down his body.

I'm wobbly and ungraceful. I kneel on him twice.

Kai Akana does not care one bit.

He's too busy stroking any part of me he can reach, muttering filthy praise, his low, melodic voice drifting through the greenhouse. When I straddle his hips, the proud jut of his cock nudging at my belly, the gardener groans and scrubs both hands down his face.

"Go easy on me. Christ, I'm gonna explode the second you

touch me, I know it."

I know the feeling. Even though I've come once already, I'm still wound tighter than a guitar string.

We both hold our breath as I notch the head against my entrance.

We let out twin groans as I sink down.

And even though this is brand new, even though I expected blood and pain and struggle, Kai's eased the way with his mouth on me, and now I'm slick and soft and ready.

"Shit." He grips my hips, squeezing tight. "Oh, shit."

I feel him throb inside me. Feel the pulse tapping in his cock.

Seriously, I feel *everything*. It's the closest I've ever been to another person, and it's so perfect I could cry.

Luckily, I'm too busy moaning and riding and clawing at Kai's chest—because yeah, that would be embarrassing.

His white t-shirt bunches in my hands, wrenched this way and that, and if the dusty path hasn't ruined the fabric, *I* definitely have. But Kai doesn't care about that either, because his head is tipped back and he's hissing low curses, while his strong hands rock me back and forth over his cock. Every time he says my name, it sounds like a prayer.

"Eden. Eden."

Our sounds echo around the greenhouse, mingling with the rushing stream and rustling leaves. The air is sticky and smells like damp soil.

"Eden, baby. *Christ*."

His thumb is on my clit. My head is spinning.

This time, the tremors start deep in my core, then roll through my body in waves. I gasp and buck my hips and try to keep going, I do, but all too soon my limbs have turned to jelly.

I collapse on Kai's chest in a sweaty heap, my body twitching with aftershocks, while he grunts and thrusts and squeezes my ass.

Even in my daze, I feel the exact moment his control snaps. The gardener's length swells inside me, stretching me even more, and then warmth floods my pussy in long spurts.

I sigh into his throat, blissed out and sticky.

It's gonna be a wobbly walk home.

Kai

⟨ornament⟩

F *ive years later*

The sunset strikes the greenhouse, filling the dome with pink and gold light. Birds of paradise chatter in the canopy, while small, brown birds scuttle across the stone paths. The stream burbles and leaves rustle and murmured voices float to me as I wind my way into the miniature rainforest.

My muscles are sore from working all day, and my t-shirt sticks to my back with sweat. Still, it's a good kind of grimy, and I'll slip into a cool shower when we get home. Bliss.

"What's this?"

"T-towel."

"Trowel."

Eden and our daughter are hunkered side by side in the undergrowth, thick as thieves as they chat together, pointing at different plants and objects. Our little girl is still learning basic words, but she can name most of the greenhouse tools.

Ish.

As I get closer, I step lightly, my hiking boots almost silent against the dirt. Birds coo a warning overhead, but my girls are oblivious—too wrapped up in each other to notice. Their heads are bowed together, one dark haired, one chestnut.

Eden's one hell of a mother. She's patient and strong, playful and caring, just like I always knew she would be. The day she showed me those two pink lines was one of the best days of my life. I whooped and spun her around in our kitchen, our laughs floating out of the open window, and thanked god for my crazy good luck.

The other thing about Eden? She's really freaking easy to spook.

Tiptoeing as close as I can on the path behind her, I wink when my daughter glances back, and hold one finger to my lips. Even though she's just a sticky, adorable little toddler, my little girl already knows how to play our games.

She turns back around, giggling.

"What's this?" Eden smiles down at her, scooching our daughter's pudgy little body even closer to her side. They're both dressed in stained old clothes, ready to play in the greenhouse dirt. Eden works here part time too, but when she brings our girl, she's strictly off duty. "What's so funny, missy?"

I lean down until my lips almost brush the top of Eden's head.

"Boo."

Her shriek sends birds clattering through the canopy, calling to each other, and our daughter explodes in bubbly laughter. I scoop her up, bouncing her against my chest. A sticky hand grabs my earlobe.

"Oh, you are such a jerk." Eden smacks at my calf before

taking my hand, and I tug her gently to her feet. "You'll pay for that later, Akana."

Hell yeah. My wife's revenge sprees are *always* fun, and they always wind up with us twined together naked.

"Good day?" Eden asks lightly as we wander back along the path. Outside the glass greenhouse, the sun burns crimson as it touches the horizon.

"The best."

Every day is the best with her. My dream.

My Eden.

III

Under Study

Description

∽◦⊱◦⊰◦∼

H e's a famous director. Older, handsome and so smart.

And he stares like he wants to eat me alive.

Don't ask me to explain it, because it makes zero sense to me. Franz Moser is surely the hottest man alive, while I'm the hottest *mess* on Kephart campus. Truly, I'm surprised I can tie my own shoelaces some days.

I'm not even a big deal in the show he's directing. I'm playing Juliet's understudy, a role that comes with no glory, and yet Mr Moser can't seem to keep his eyes off me.

When I walk in a room, he stares. When I leave, he follows. And when I'm cold, he drapes me in his sweater.

Is this seriously happening? Is the gorgeous older director

falling for the curvy college student?

Or am I caught up in my own daydreams?

Sylvie

It's so easy to fall in love backstage in a theater. It's the perfect environment.

First of all, there's the camaraderie; the feeling on every play and production that the cast and crew are all one big tight-knit family. Everyone knows everyone's business, and we live in each other's pockets for a few short months. We see each other's highs and lows; we see each other first thing in the morning, yawning wide, and last thing at night, sore but satisfied. It's intimate as hell.

With so much closeness, sparks are quick to fly.

Then there's the theater itself. The backstage space. Kephart College has a huge auditorium, filled with the latest tech, but there are still plenty of nooks and crannies behind the scenes. Lots of places to hide, giggling quietly; plenty of dark corners to tuck away with someone, fumbling in the shadows.

Sneaking around is fun, or so I've been told. And theaters are perfect for illicit hookups. So there's that.

Even so, at twenty two years old, and in my last year as a

drama major, I somehow missed all that. Never snuck behind the drapes with a hot actor or a sound technician; never raised the temperature in the costume store with a member of the stage crew. Never sighed after our stage manager, wishing he'd boss me around in bed as well as backstage.

In fact, I never had a crush, period. Until *him*.

Our much older, very handsome, *famous* guest director. The man who burst into our department as the star of our last semester; the man who makes butterflies explode inside me every time he looks my way.

The man who I should stay away from now, even as I'm drawn to him like a moth to a light. The man who's way out of my league.

Two months together, working on *Romeo and Juliet*. Two months of keeping my crush a secret.

…Oh, boy. This is gonna be tricky.

* * *

"Alright, everyone: Act One, Scene Five. Our doomed lovers meet for the first time. From the top, please."

Our director's voice is deep and rasping, tinged with a faint Austrian accent. As the leads hurry to the stage, play scripts clutched in their hands, I suppress a secret shiver and slide further down in my seat, forcing myself to look at anyone but him.

This man gives me the tingles so bad.

Franz Moser: famous director and silver fox. He should come with a warning label.

We're in the Kephart auditorium, and the stage is empty for our rehearsals—though white tape marks on the floor show where the scenery will eventually go. The ceiling soars high overhead, and the whole cast is adrift in a sea of blue velvet chairs.

We're all spread through the first few rows, paging through scripts or sneakily tapping away at our laptops, working on other assignments while we wait for our turn onstage.

The leads launch into the scene, and the rest of the world fades away as I mouth Juliet's lines along silently. As her understudy, I need to have every word memorized, even if I never get to say them onstage. I'm trying not to be bitter about that, but I won't lie—when we got our roles last week, my heart sank.

What's that saying—always the bridesmaid, never the bride? Well, this is my third time playing the understudy to the leading lady. My third time *almost* reaching the limelight, but missing by a single inch.

I'm good enough for a main role. They wouldn't keep choosing me to be the understudy otherwise, because there's always a real chance the lead could get sick and I'd have to do the whole run. So they *know* I have it in me—they see it too.

But for whatever reason, I'm never the first choice for the role. Always the back-up instead. So… here we go again.

"You kiss by th'book," Juliet says up onstage, teasing her Romeo. She flips her hair, smiling coquettishly at her new love interest, and *ugh*, that's not how I'd play that line at all. Where is her uncertainty? Where's the panic that comes when a crush takes you over, body and soul? She's never felt like this before, so why is she so damn confident?

"Sylvie," a low voice rumbles, raising the hairs on the back of my neck. When I inhale sharply and turn, I find the handsome director looming above me in the row.

He's tall and broad; dark haired with strands of silver at his temples. Franz Moser is good looking in a craggy sort of way—like a horny sculptor hewed him out of a cliff side.

He's dressed today in dark jeans and a soft gray sweater that looks more expensive than my whole closet combined, the sleeves pushed to his elbows to reveal toned forearms dusted with dark hair.

He's got to be around twice my age, and here I am squirming in my blue velvet chair at the mere sight of him. Clearly, I have issues I hadn't even clocked until now.

"Oops!" Rocketing to my feet, I shuffle back to let him by. Someone barks out a laugh in the row behind, turning it too late into a cough.

Yeah, yeah, this man turns me into a bumbling goon. That has become abundantly clear over the first week of rehearsals, but my fellow acting students still titter into their play scripts. Can't even blame them, really.

"Sorry, Mr Moser."

"Franz is fine." His faint smile is knowing, and a light glints in his dark eyes. When the director sinks into the seat beside mine, my insides turn to nervous jelly. Oh god, he's so *big* in that chair, all long limbs and elbows propped on arm rests. "I'm just here to pick your brain about Juliet. I thought we could watch these scenes together and compare notes. Understudy can be a thankless role, I know."

My legs wobble as I sink back down, and the back of my neck is hot. I can *feel* all those eyes on me—all the eyes that should be watching the leads onstage, and instead are glued to me, waiting for me to blush bright red next to this handsome director. It's only been a week, and already my radioactive crush on this man is the stuff of campus legend.

138

Wish I could leave them disappointed, but... yeah, I'm definitely crimson right now.

"Sure." My fingers tremble as I smooth out the play script, thankfully turned to the correct page for this scene. Up on stage, the leads stumble through their lines, checking their scripts again and again for the right words.

That's fair. We're only a week into rehearsals, and this is Shakespeare. It's not the easiest material to learn. And if *I* already have most of Acts One and Two memorized, that's because I'm a giant theater dweeb with no other hobbies and a tragic dream of impressing the man next to me.

"Juliet is young," Franz notes, shifting to get comfortable in his seat. The wood creaks beneath his bulk, and I can't help glancing at the way his muscled thighs press against his jeans; the swell of his hard chest beneath his sweater; the understated style of his watch; hell, just... all of him. "She's younger than Romeo. But she's still the wisest of the pair; the most emotionally mature of them both. She understands the risks they're taking better than he does."

My snort echoes through the auditorium, and Franz's mouth twitches as I blush even harder. He glances at me, eyebrows raised, like he wants me to explain my outburst.

"Well, yeah," I mutter, embarrassed at my own awkwardness. Maybe if I keep my eyes glued to the stage, watching the leads circle each other, tension building, I can block out my own nonsense. Surreptitiously, I wipe my clammy palms on my leggings.

"But that's true of most heterosexual relationships, wouldn't you say? Women are used to carrying a heavier load. We're the ones who risk having rumors spread about us if we get close to the wrong man. We're the ones who could get pregnant and find ourselves alone. Of course Juliet is nervous—she's falling in love, yes, but she also knows that men aren't always a good bet. Even the ones that *seem* great at first glance. We're all raised to be cautious," I finish, wishing I could shrink down into a tiny ball and disappear. The velvet scuffs against my back as I try to do just that.

Because what am I doing? Franz Moser didn't ask for a basic bitch feminist lecture. I snorted, and he looked politely concerned. Now I have the horrible sensation of being exposed—like I've cracked open my rib cage and given the handsome director a sneak peek at my squishy insides. It's all way too vulnerable for a Monday morning.

There's a long pause beside me, until I can't bear not looking any longer. A stolen glance shows the director leaning back in his chair, stroking his firm jaw, deep in thought. A faint frown pinches his dark eyebrows together, and his freshly shaved chin rasps beneath his hand, even though it's only mid-morning.

Romeo and Juliet rush together onstage, arms twining around each other, like they can't bear to be parted even after a single meeting. I used to think love at first sight was a stupid idea, but now…

"That is a wonderful insight," Franz says at last, and I practically melt into a puddle on the floor in relief. "I'm glad I picked your brain, Sylvie. I'll have to do it again. We all have blind spots and, well…"

He waves at his large, older, immaculately dressed, *male* body, as if to make his point. And you know what? It really, really does.

What would this man know about how precarious life can be for a woman? Intellectually he might understand, but how could he know how it *feels*?

My tongue unsticks from the roof of my mouth just as Franz stands up. He looms over me, blocking out the ceiling lights high above.

"Any time," I mumble, my cheeks still burning hot.

As the director shuffles his magnificent bulk back along the row, I'm surrounded by gossipy whispers. I hold my play script up in front of my unseeing eyes, pretending I can't hear them.

Franz

৵৵ঌৡৢ৵৵

The early weeks of rehearsal are always rocky, in my experience. There are the nerves that come with a new production, when all the actors secretly think that they will never, ever manage to learn their lines, and will surely be kicked off the show before they ultimately wind up living in a cardboard box under a bridge. Actors are nothing if not dramatic.

Then there's all the posturing as everyone figures out the new social dynamics. Every production is a microcosm—a miniature society that needs to function so that the tension stays onstage where it belongs. Theater is home to plenty of big egos, and the first few weeks of rehearsal can be a strain as everyone figures out their place.

And of course there's the new space, new cast mates, new schedule to adapt to. I don't blame anyone for feeling frazzled, especially these college students with so little life experience. They've got other classes to balance with this too, and I don't envy them that for one minute.

You know what's not normal, though? The rockiness that comes when the director can't keep his damn eyes off a certain understudy. *That* is not standard at all.

And I've tried to keep away from Sylvie. Tried to ensure that we don't speak too much; that I don't seek her out too often. I've made sure that I sit at least a few rows away each day, and limit the amount of times I turn to glance at her each hour, mentally tallying them up in my brain.

Even so... people have noticed. They'd have to be blind not to.

Because I'm losing my goddamn mind over that curvy college student.

She's nothing like the people I'm used to back home where I settled in London. She's not curt or clipped; her humor is not biting. She's not hardened by the big city, constantly wearing invisible armor as if she has to prove herself over and over.

No, Sylvie is... soft. Sweet and shy. She's kind and considerate, but with zero filter between her brain and her lips. Whatever she thinks, she says, before blushing bright red and staring bug-eyed at the wall. They'd eat her alive back in the West End.

God, she's adorable.

And sexy, too. Petite and curvy, with big blue eyes and flyaway blonde hair that my hands itch to plunge into. Fuck, I just want to pull Sylvie into my lap and pet her until she squirms. Want to tickle her waist and growl filthy things in her ear and lick the soft column of her neck—never mind that I'm twice her age.

No wonder everyone's noticed. Ever since I laid eyes on her, I'm unhinged. Don't recognize myself.

The scene finishes up on stage, and silence spreads through

the auditorium before I notice a beat too late. Clearing my throat, I applaud quickly to hide my distraction, and the other cast members join in too until the sound bounces off the walls.

"Good," I call at last, once my head is on straight. "Very good. Tomorrow we'll move on to the next scene, but I'd like you both to keep drilling those lines. We want to get off book as soon as possible so that we can move on to blocking."

The leads nod eagerly, both visibly relieved, and a few others stand and shuffle along their rows. We're rehearsing a fight scene after the break, and the young men are already grinning at each other, rolling their necks and puffing up their chests. This session promises to be messy.

I should focus. Need all my attention on this next scene.

But when Sylvie slides out of her row and heads out of the auditorium doors, I push to my feet to follow. Though she doesn't seem to realize it, I'm tugged after her on an invisible string.

"Ten minutes," I call as I stride down the center aisle. Whispers follow in my wake, and I'm an old fool, but I can't change direction now. Can't help following wherever Sylvie leads. "Don't be late back."

I'm talking to myself as much as anyone, squinting in the bright spring sunshine as I step outside. Fresh air hits me like a slap, cold and invigorating, and I step out just in time to see Sylvie's blonde hair whip around a corner.

I should turn around. Should go back inside and keep far away from my curvy student.

But chest drumming, I follow.

* * *

Kephart College is pretty in the spring—though I suppose anywhere with sunshine and blossoming trees looks good after a long, dark winter. The last few months have been especially bad too, with rough winds, constant rain, and dark clouds camped out over the London rooftops.

Here, though, despite all the concrete and paved paths, the ocean sparkles blue in the distance, and emerald green grass covers the steep cliff that rises above the campus. A greenhouse perches on top like a glass hat.

It's beautiful. But I can't bring myself to look anywhere except at the young woman flopping down on a wooden bench beneath a tree in the campus courtyard.

Pigeons peck at the bare stone beneath the bench, like they're hoping to magic up some dropped crumbs by will alone. And a gentle breeze ruffles the pink and white blossoms on the tree branches—the same breeze that lifts the ends of Sylvie's blonde hair, dancing it across her shoulders.

She's in a blue t-shirt from an old production of Guys & Dolls, but as I stroll up behind her, Sylvie shivers and hugs her arms close. It may be sunny, but it's a weak, watery sunshine—one that barely casts a shadow as I stand behind the bench.

"You're cold."

Sylvie leaps about a foot into the air, yelping with surprise. Though it makes me a bastard, I can't help grinning as she wheels around.

"I—you—"

She's adorable when she splutters, her cheeks already pink. But now that she's turned to face me, the goosebumps on her bare arms are even more obvious. The hard beads of her nipples betray her too, pressing against her t-shirt to declare that it's freezing out here.

145

"You should wrap up warmer," I say, tugging down my own sleeves. The pigeons coo and peck at my boots, and I nudge them away gently before drawing my sweater up over my head.

"Oh, Mr Moser—wait—"

"It's Franz." Somehow, when I emerge back into the fresh air, Sylvie is even redder than before. She's nibbling on her bottom lip, staring wide-eyed at the gray sweater in my hand. I hold it out, and she makes a tiny squeak like she can't quite believe her eyes. What I'm doing. What I'm *offering*.

"Go on." Keeping my tone level, I try not to sound too eager. "Put it on. I don't want my cast to be cold."

Least of all Sylvie. Not when I could keep her warm, wrapping her up in my clothing. In my scent. Not when the beast inside me purrs with satisfaction at the thought of her draped in my sweater.

And I said that to soothe her, to help allay her fears, but Sylvie looks strangely... disappointed. Her shoulders slump, and her smile at me is resigned. Still, she plucks the gray sweater from my hands and holds it up to inspect it before shrugging it on.

"I didn't slop coffee down myself," I tease. "You can trust me, Sylvie."

She shakes her head, amused, even as her palms smooth down the sweater front. Like she can't stop touching the soft wool.

"Hardly. I was just... clothes don't always fit me, so I..."

She trails off, pressing her lips together.

Down by our feet, the pigeons coo at each other, ruffling up their feathers in warning. Fighting over their imaginary crumbs.

"This sweater fits, though. It fits just fine." My voice sounds rough; unbalanced. Can you blame me? It's affecting me more than I thought it would—seeing Sylvie wear my clothes. "You should keep that, sweetheart. Wear it for the rest of the day."

Let everyone see that you're mine.

I shove that thought away, suddenly glad there's a bench between us. God knows what I'd do otherwise, because my hands are itching to reach out and pull this curvy student close; to clutch the understudy against my chest and feel her heartbeat throb against mine. To draw the scent of her skin into my lungs.

So out of line. And thank god for inconvenient benches, because so far, I can brush off most of this interaction as reasonably normal.

We both came outside for some fresh air in the break. That's normal; that's fine.

I saw Sylvie was cold and offered her my sweater. The rest of the cast will surely gossip like hens, but that's not *so* unreasonable either. I haven't crossed any lines.

Yet.

"Soft," Sylvie mumbles, rubbing the sleeves together. I watch without blinking, my heart beating way too hard against my ribs. God, what is it about this girl? "Thanks, Mr Moser."

"It's Franz." My smile is strained. "If you're wearing my sweater, surely you can call me by my name."

Sylvie wets her lips, unsure.

My abs tighten.

Say it. Say it.

"Alright," she says at last, her mouth curving into a secret smile all for me. "Thank you, Franz. We'd better get back, hadn't we?"

Yes, we had.

I don't trust myself alone with her any longer.

Sylvie

❧

The dorm is noisy as hell when I get home after dinner, the straps of my backpack digging into my shoulders. Don't get me wrong—I *love* being in shows, love working on productions, but the long hours of sitting in the audience make me creaky as hell.

Then there are all the lines to memorize. Lines I may never get to say—Juliet's whole story, committed to my brain but then left there in the dark. Plus the blocking, the warm ups and cool downs, the notes, the time spent helping the crew to paint flats and sew costumes. It all adds up into one huge, crazy commitment that I wouldn't give up for all the treasure in the world, but that leaves me coming home to my dorm each night exhausted.

But I'm the only one here dragging my feet tonight, it seems. Bursts of laughter float out of the common room, and music blasts in the showers as I walk past, breathing in a lungful of shampoo-scented mist. It may be a Monday, but at Kephart College, that stops no one. Any night can be a good night with the right attitude.

My dorm room is empty when I get in. No surprises there. My roommate is dating a local in town, and she spends basically every spare minute at his apartment.

Guess I can't blame her, no matter how lonely it makes me feel sometimes. Our lumpy twin beds aren't the most luxurious things you've ever seen.

Still, when I drop my backpack on the floor and face plant on the saggy mattress, the groan that bursts out of me comes from deep within my soul. Every muscle is tired; every bone in my body creaks. There's a headache pulsing behind my right eye, and I still need to do the reading for my regular classes tomorrow.

So. Freaking. Tired.

But...

The scent of cedar and masculine soap fills my nose. It takes me way too long to realize that it's coming from Franz's sweater, from the neckline. When I flopped forward, the big gust of air blew his scent into my face.

And holy shit, this is the best thing I've smelled. *He's* the best thing I've ever smelled. Wish I could bottle that man's scent and dab it on my wrists. Wish I could spritz it on my pillow before going to bed each night. What kind of crazy pheromones do they have in Austria anyways?

God help me, but I wriggle. Biting my lip, holding my breath, I ground down into his soft woolen sweater, and... wriggle. And it's soft and tickly and smells so good, and now there's a weird throbbing sensation in my lower belly.

Should have given the sweater back at the end of rehearsal. Should have handed it back and scuttled away, and hidden my blushes away from the director's knowing gaze. But instead, when I offered to give the sweater back at the end of the day, Franz gave me this *look*.

This long, heated look.

A look that said: *Keep it on.*

And I could no more have disobeyed that look than I could have flown into the sun. So… here I am. Wearing my older, handsome director's gray sweater and sniffing the collar; grinding against the soft wool like I could work his scent right into my cells. Tired and aching and clearly losing my freaking mind, because I should be cracking open tomorrow's reading right now, not… not…

My breath catches as I jam a hand beneath myself, stroking down the front of my body. If I squeeze my eyes shut and focus really hard, I can pretend that it's a much bigger hand, with squared knuckles and long fingers. A manly hand, ending in an expensive watch and a forearm dusted with dark hairs.

"Franz." His name puffs out of me on an exhale, and I just need to say it out loud. Need to confess this *somewhere*; confess that my body goes loopy every time our famous guest director looks my way. Because if I ever whispered that fact to a real, live person, they'd only look at me with pity.

No sane person would put us together. No sane person would ever think I'd have a chance with that man.

Because he's older and stern and smart and successful, while I'm a shy, goofy college student who can never seem to land a leading role. He's sculpted from pure muscle; I'm squishy *everywhere.* This pairing makes no sense.

And yet… he lent me this sweater, and wouldn't take it back. And I swear, every time he saw me in it today, the director got this hungry look in his eyes.

"Franz," I whisper again, sliding my hand beneath the

waistband of my leggings. And thank god my roommate is never around, because if I don't scratch this itch in the next twenty seconds, I'm going to explode.

I'm wound tight. Hot and flustered. Have been all day—no, all *week*—and it's so much worse with his scent in my lungs and his sweater on my body and the memory of his deep, rough voice ringing in my ears. My pulse throbs between my legs, aching and insistent.

Sweetheart. Did Franz Moser really call me sweetheart? Or did I imagine that?

Maybe he calls everyone sweetheart. Maybe he gives out sweaters like candy. Maybe none of this means anything, and I'm making a fool out of myself, even here where I'm all alone.

Flopping onto my back, I suck in a shaky breath. I should stop, shouldn't build my own hopes up like this by picturing a man like Franz wanting me, but I can't help it. The way he came and sat by me in rehearsals, and truly valued what I said… the way he followed me outside on the break and then fussed over me getting cold…

The triumphant, possessive glint in his eye when I first shrugged on his sweater…

"*Oh.*" Muffling my noises against his sleeve, I circle my fingers faster, stroking the achy, slick flesh between my legs. My thigh muscles twitch; my spine arches off the mattress. I'm sweaty under my clothes, breathing hard, all quivery and desperate, but I can't get there. Can't chase myself higher. Can't—

"Shit. God. Shit." My whispers carry across the empty dorm room, past the Broadway posters and photos of my friends on the walls. My roommate never bothered to decorate her half of the room, so the wall coverings abruptly run out halfway, turning to scuffed white paint. Seeing that drop off has always been so depressing.

My wrist twinges from the weird angle, half jammed inside my leggings but my fingers move faster between my legs. I *need* this.

Every minute in that rehearsal room with Franz sets a restless need squirming in my belly.

And in the end, that's the thought that gets me there. That's what makes my blood flush hot and my belly clench: the thought of Franz up on that stage, addressing the whole auditorium in that deep, rasping voice. The way his eyes always seem to track to me—then stay there, heating up. The rumble of his words in my bones.

And the thought of what I *wish* he'd do after: drag me into the darkness at the side of the stage once everyone else has gone, press that big, strong body against mine and crowd me back until I hit a wall.

Kiss me and bite me and shove his leg between mine, ordering me in that clipped Austrian accent to ride his thigh until I come.

There's more, too, but I lose the thread of my thoughts. Lose track of everything except the frantic thud of my pulse in my ears, the maddening stroke of my fingers between my legs, the tingling and gasping and how my whole body goes rigid, the director's name on my lips.

I come so hard the rest of the room fades away. Come so hard it could be minutes or even hours later when I collapse back onto the mattress in a breathless puddle, and I couldn't tell.

My heart throbs in time with my clit.

Oh, boy.

Franz. Is he thinking about me too? Am I special to him at all… or is this all in my head?

Daniel is so blinded by attraction... and respect to him at all. He is proud of all my grades.

Franz

The next day in rehearsal, Sylvie won't meet my eye. She slinks into the auditorium with her head ducked and shoulders raised, then slides into a seat five rows behind me and buries her nose in her play script.

But all around her, whispers start up. Because Sylvie's wearing my sweater again. She's bundled in the soft gray wool, swamped in the fabric, and I'm so fucking pleased with that sight that I can't help staring over my shoulder, chest thumping hard.

"Mr Moser? Um. Franz?"

It takes all my focus, but I yank my attention back to the student hovering in my row. He's thin and gangly, with brown hair and wide, constantly-surprised eyes, and he's playing Mercutio.

"Yes? What is it, Daniel?"

Though it's been a week already, these students are still tiptoeing around me, always careful. Not because I'm some tyrant, but simply because in this rehearsal space, my word is law.

They'll all relax eventually, loosening up enough to tease me, even, but for now…

Being treated like some kind of ogre is exhausting.

"I, um." Daniel clears his throat, his Adam's apple bobbing. "I have a question about the fight scene we blocked yesterday?"

I nod. "Go on."

And as Daniel chatters away, asking about stage combat techniques, half of my brain tunes out to focus on the young woman five rows behind me.

Sylvie's sitting alone this morning, though she has plenty of friends in the cast and crew. She looked tired when she first slipped into the auditorium, with dark shadows beneath her eyes. Like she didn't sleep well last night.

I know the feeling.

Though I don't turn my head, though we're surrounded by other students and distractions, I swear I hear every rustle and sigh that Sylvie makes. Can pick out the crinkle of *her* play script from among all the others; can tell when she unscrews her daily thermos of peppermint tea, the lid squeaking gently. Does her breath taste like peppermint after her first sip? Does she inhale the steam, letting it waft against her cheeks?

Even though I answer all of Daniel's questions, keeping pace easily with the conversation, most of me is five rows away. I'm not proud of that fact, by the way. I'm *alarmed*.

Because… what is this young woman doing to me? Over a week has passed now, and my obsession shows no sign of fading. If anything, it grows each day.

"Thanks, Mr Moser."

I wave Daniel off, shaken by the strength of my own fixation with Sylvie five rows behind. Sylvie, who's dressed in my sweater again. Sylvie, who I dreamed of last night, tossing and turning in my rented apartment by the sea.

"Alright, everyone." Clapping once, I push to my feet, turning around to survey the actors grouped in the rows. They look tired but eager, clutching giant takeout cups of coffee and already paging through their scripts, the papers trembling in their over-caffeinated hands.

"Act Two, Scene Two," I say, my voice echoing around the auditorium. This whole room was designed to carry sound. "The famous balcony scene. Romeo risks death to sneak into the Capulet garden and find his new love."

This isn't the first time I've directed this play, but it's certainly the first time in my life that I've understood the risks Romeo takes. Would I risk life and limb for a few stolen moments with a new love? A week ago, I would have scoffed at the idea. But now that I've met Sylvie?

In a heartbeat.

And seriously, what the hell is wrong with me? Why am I so head over heels for a young woman I met only last week; why does my pulse spike whenever she's near?

Maybe it's the jet lag from London. Or something in the Kephart water.

Or maybe it's—

"Love at first sight," I remind the leads as they hurry up the steps on either side of the stage. "You've both fallen in love at first sight. And you've fallen so deeply, so recklessly, that you're risking your lives for a few stolen moments together."

Don't turn around. Don't look at her.

I'm twice Sylvie's age, after all. Even if *I'm* gone for her, even if I hear the goddamn wedding march every time I glance her way, that doesn't mean she reciprocates—and I'd hate to ever make her uncomfortable.

"But soft," Romeo says onstage. "What light through yonder window breaks? It is the east, and Juliet is the sun."

* * *

"Understudies. Your turn at Act Three, Scene Five."

Three hours later, the auditorium is stuffily hot, and someone has propped open the doors in hopes of a breeze. Even though it's spring, even though the sea was choppy in the distance when I stepped outside during the last break, this room is hot enough that all my actors are wilting.

They sag in their blue velvet seats, fanning themselves with their scripts. The energy is draining away quickly, and we still have an hour left of rehearsal. Poor Juliet is practically draped over a friend in exhaustion, and that's my cue to change our plan quickly.

So why not give Sylvie a chance to rehearse? Understudying is hard—she needs to learn her own ensemble role, plus all of Juliet's lines and blocking, all on the off-chance that she'll get a chance to perform it. And sure enough, even though everyone else is tired, Sylvie jumps to her feet eagerly.

I trail her to the stage, the wooden steps creaking beneath my bulk. And it takes an embarrassingly long amount of time before I frown and drag my eyes away from Sylvie, finally realizing that we're alone onstage.

"Where is Tomas?"

The understudy for Romeo is usually diligent, arriving early for every rehearsal. "Stomach flu," someone calls from the back, and I grunt and nod.

Fine. This will still be worthwhile for Sylvie.

"Jack," I call, scanning the huddled actors for our lead. Yes, he's been playing Romeo all morning, but he might have to act alongside Sylvie onstage one day. It will be good for them both to rehearse together.

"He went to meet his advisor," someone else calls, and I turn away from the crowd, irritation prickling the back of my neck.

No, I'm not a tyrant, and I don't stomp and yell like some directors. But I still expect full attendance and commitment, and Jack and I will have words about this.

Sylvie deserves to rehearse her scenes whenever she gets a chance. And right now, seeing the disappointment cloud her blue eyes, seeing her shoulders slump in resignation, I could wring Jack's unreliable neck.

"I'll read for Romeo." My words are quiet, just for Sylvie, but the first row of actors must hear, because whispers ripple through our audience. Suddenly, they don't look nearly as tired as a moment ago. They're all perked up in their chairs, eager and attentive. Hungry for gossip. "But I'm not off book, I'm afraid."

"Amateur hour," she teases softly, offering her own play script to me. Of course she's learned her lines by heart already. Sylvie is committed as hell.

And I realize as soon as we launch into the scene: this was a mistake. Of all the scenes we could have rehearsed, of all the blocking we could have tried, this is possibly the worst scene I could have chosen.

In my defense, I didn't realize it would be *me* up here, running these lines with Sylvie. Moving through the blocking, taking her in my arms and clutching her to my chest.

Because in the play, this is the morning after Romeo and Juliet's wedding night. They've been intimate already; they kiss and touch each other freely, and not only that, but with a desperate fear that they might never get another chance.

As I draw Sylvie against my front, as I feel her soft curves against my chest, I know how they feel.

Keep it together, I warn myself, sticking to the script, even as my blood heats and my gut twists and every cell in my body cries out to get her closer, closer. *Don't scare the poor thing. Keep to the script.*

"Wilt thou be gone?" Sylvie says, her voice wobbling. Like she's knocked off kilter by this as much as I am. "It is not yet near day."

And what I'd fucking give to have Sylvie beg me to stay with her like this. What I'd give to draw her close and cup her cheek and breathe her peppermint tea breath into my lungs. Jack doesn't know how lucky he is—nor Tomas.

If I played Romeo opposite Sylvie, I'd drill this scene ten times a day. Any excuse to get close to her, I'd take it.

The scene moves on, with Juliet first begging Romeo to stay, then urging him to go as their situation becomes more dangerous. And all the while, between every line of dialog, we cling together, heartbeats pounding in time.

I can *feel* it.

Feel her heat, her shuddering breaths, the frantic slam of Sylvie's heart against her rib cage. Like she's as tormented by this as I am. Like she's not just acting either—she's also desperate to get near.

Up on this stage, with Sylvie in my arms, the rest of the world fades away. The whispering, wide-eyed audience; the distant chatter of campus floating through the open doors; the shadowy silence of the wings. There's nothing in the whole universe except the soft press of Sylvie's waist under my palm, and the heat of her body through *my* sweater, and the way her lips part when she gazes up at me.

The kiss is scripted, for the record. I'm not *that* much of a monster as to steal an unwanted kiss from Sylvie like this, and I keep strictly to the script, but…

When the time comes, I kiss her harder than an actor should. Kiss her deeper, longer, with more hunger and desperation than I ought to, gripping her close to me and groaning softly against her lips. And I'm not trying to cross any lines—if anything, I'm battling to rein myself in—but the second our lips brush, the last shreds of logic fly out of my brain.

Sylvie sighs and melts against me, kissing me back. When her pearly little teeth scrape my bottom lip, nipping me there, I get hard enough to drill through granite.

She wants me too.

That thought rings though me like a bell, clear and strong, and when I finally stagger back to rasp the next line, it repeats over and over in a loop in my brain.

She wants me too. She wants me too.

The audience hums below us, electrified by the scene they just witnessed. The way their director clutched his understudy close and kissed her like he needed air from her lungs to breathe. The way my body responded to Sylvie's, my cock pressing against my jeans and my heart beating so hard, it must be visible from rows away.

Sylvie says the rest of Juliet's lines with a quaver in her voice and a permanent pink stain on her cheeks.

I stumble through the rest of the scene alongside her, like my whole world didn't just turn upside down.

She wants me too. Sylvie wants me too.

But first, I must let her come to me.

Sylvie

≈⊙≋⊙≈

The next few weeks are so freaking confusing, I could scream.

On the one hand, rehearsals are ramping up. Everyone's getting off book, leaving their play scripts on their seats when they're called to stage, and only occasionally calling for a line. Sets are built in the workshop backstage, and we've all helped to sew and paint and move boxes of props. The excitement of our opening night creeps closer every day, until there's a constant buzz of adrenaline in the auditorium. This is the best thing about theater. It's like receiving a steady electric shock—in the best way.

And I *am* excited about all that, I swear. I really am.

But mostly, I'm trying to make sense of our director.

Because all those weeks ago when Franz rehearsed that scene with me on stage, kissing me like he wanted to devour me, body and soul, kissing me until my head swam and my belly quivered…

Maybe it's dumb and naive of me, but I was so sure Franz

161

meant it. Was so sure that it wasn't all acting; that he really is as drawn to me as I am to him. Like an idiot, I thought: no one can act *that* well, surely? No one can force their heart to beat harder, so hard it rattled his chest? No one can fake the way his pupils blew wide?

But since then... nothing. No secret trysts. No Austrian silver fox serenading me below my dorm window. Nada. And now I feel like a giant idiot. An inexperienced moron who got daydreams mixed up with reality.

"Places," Franz calls, clapping his hands from his seat four rows back. We're rehearsing a big fight scene this morning, the scuffle between Capulets and Montagues that opens the play, and as part of my ensemble role, I'm one of the bodies in the background. Generic Woman Screaming. Still, at least this is *my* role and no one else's.

As we all take our places on stage, Franz's gaze rests on me for a long moment, sending heat prickling down my spine. Jaw tight, I stare at the floor and refuse to meet his eye.

If I read everything all wrong, if I kidded myself that my crush might be returned, that's not Franz's fault. I do know that.

But that doesn't mean I can bear seeing the neutral expression in his eyes—the one he's worn since our big stage kiss. Sometimes, I think there's maybe a flicker of heat there too, especially on days when I wear his sweater, but... that's the kind of wishful thinking that made me an object of gossip in the first place.

And boy do these actors gossip. They don't mean to be cruel or anything—it's just the way things are when everyone is thrown together in an intense environment for a few weeks. Hopes are raised then dashed, hearts are broken, and everyone around knows it.

Some of them even pat my shoulder when I look especially dejected in the mornings, and Loren, the girl who's playing Juliet, brought me a candy bar to rehearsal yesterday afternoon.

So... yeah. It's sweet of them all, but I'm chock full up of pity, and I'm not about to make a scene over the director who unknowingly crushed my heart. Looking away and keeping my distance is just easier.

"Gregory, o' my word, we'll not carry coals."

The opening line rings through the auditorium as two Capulets enter onstage. They're not in costume yet, both dressed in jeans and t-shirts, but the prop swords are slung on their belts. I'm in the background looking busy, just a Verona woman going about her daily life.

Even so, there's a tell tale heat creeping over my skin that says Franz is watching me. *Why?* I'm barely part of this scene, and I'm doing my job just fine, thank you very much. I may not be leading lady material, but I'm perfectly capable of ensemble work.

"Do you bite your thumb at us, sir?"

The Capulets and Montagues square off in the middle of the stage. Still, even as insults are exchanged and swords are drawn, the heat of Franz's gaze never leaves me.

When I can't bear it any longer, when sparks are crackling under my skin and my body is so freaking *aware* that I jump at the slightest breeze from the wings, I finally risk a glance into the audience.

The director rests his chin on one fist, frowning straight at me. Even from all the way up here, toward the back of the stage, I can see the frustrated glint in his dark eyes.

A shiver coasts down my bare arms. I'm not wearing his gray

sweater today—only a white t-shirt and navy leggings. Still, Franz glares up at me like he wants to eat me alive. Do the other actors see it too? There are quiet murmurs on the other side of stage, and one of the Montagues turns to look at me.

We get through the scene, even with Franz staring at me non-stop. By the time we're done, the fighters panting with their swords held loosely in their hands, my cheeks are stained permanent red. My insides are all jittery, and this man makes no *sense*.

My chin wobbles.

I might cry.

"Excellent," Franz says, glancing down at the notes in his lap. "We'll break for lunch there."

I'm zooming off the stage before his sentence is even finished, feet pounding down the creaky wooden steps. Franz's dark head jerks up, whipping in my direction, but I'm already hurrying toward the doors. To fresh air; to freedom.

"Sylvie," Franz calls, his deep voice carrying easily through the auditorium, clipped with alarm, but I pretend I didn't hear it. The heavy door swings open under my palms.

"Sylvie—"

The door slams shut behind me, and I suck in a lungful of fresh spring air. My legs wobble as I set off around the corner, and I don't know where I'm going except... away.

* * *

Franz catches up to me in the campus rose garden. Of course he does.

"Sylvie. What's wrong?"

When his deep voice rumbles through the spring air, making

my nerves skitter and my heart leap, I puff out a breath and wheel around to face him.

Franz strides toward me, those long legs carrying him faster than I could ever manage. The director looks more tired and crankier than usual today, with his dark eyebrows pinched in a permanent frown. It's a warm day, and his broad torso is wrapped in a moss green Henley that brings out the gold flecks in his brown eyes.

"Nothing's wrong," I say, desperately trying to believe my own words. But spending that whole scene with his eyes on me has set me horribly off kilter, and now I'm all sad and raw and confused.

Because... *why?* Why stare at me like that if our stage kiss meant nothing?

Why keep his distance ever since if he liked me too?

Why mess with my head like this, chasing me one moment and stepping back the next? Why can't anything ever be freaking *simple?*

"You ran off." The words scrape out of Franz's throat, and his gaze roves over me as we square off in the rose garden. As if he's starving for every detail of me, even after everything. As if he's calmed by having me close. "Talk to me, sweetheart."

Sweetheart. There it is again.

And I can't make sense of this man. Do I even want to?

"I just... needed a minute." There: that's true, but vague. I'm not lying, but I'm not opening myself up for heartache either. "I'll be back before the break's over, don't worry."

Franz makes a rough sound in the back of his throat and shakes his head. "I'll always worry about you, Sylvie."

My laugh is harsh. Startled. The director's frown deepens even more, and he takes a single step closer to me on the stone path. Rose bushes are chest high all around us, but it's too early in the year for their flowers. Just as well, probably. The last thing I need is to get carried away by my imagination again.

"I've been giving you space," Franz says slowly, like he wants me to understand. "Space to come to me. To choose me for yourself. But don't doubt that I'm waiting for you, Sylvie."

Thump, goes my frazzled heart. *Thump, thump, thump.*

He's been waiting for me? Giving me space? Why would he do that?

As though he can read the confusion in my eyes, Franz sighs and reaches out to tug gently on a lock of my hair. Butterflies explode in my belly at his simple touch.

"I'm twice your age, Sylvie. And I'm directing this play. You can't see why I might need to be cautious about this? Why it needs to be your decision to move forward?"

Those brown eyes are so, so handsome. And the silver strands at his temples; the dark stubble that coats his jaw by mid-morning each day; his broad shoulders and toned forearms. Everything about this man is freaking perfect, and when the breeze wafts his soap and cedar scent to me, my knees wobble beneath me.

Can't believe this. Can't believe my ears.

He wants me? Franz Moser, famous director and silver fox extraordinaire, really wants me? *Me?* Sylvie the hot mess college student?

"I thought... I didn't... didn't know..."

Franz lets me mumble, swaying on my feet on the stone path. Pigeons strut between the rose bushes, and seagulls screech from nearby rooftops. It's a blue sky day, with a fresh, floral breeze and clumps of white cloud skidding high above. The ocean sparkles in the distance.

He wants me? The jigsaw reassembles in my brain, reframing the last few weeks, and the new knowledge spreads through me until I'm all warm and gooey inside, freaking *desperate* to finally get this man alone.

"My dorm is over there," I whisper, pointing at a nearby building. Franz's smile is slow and heated, and for the first time in weeks, the frown melts away from his forehead.

"Rehearsals start again in five," he points out, but already it's like a weight has lifted from his shoulders. He's standing taller, breathing freer. "But come to me after. If this is what you want."

"It is."

I say it way, way too fast, but Franz growls in approval and steps forward, brushing a kiss against my forehead before backing away. That tiny brush of contact nearly overloads my senses.

"I'll be waiting," he repeats. "Don't doubt that again, Sylvie."

Oh my *god*.

My insides explode into glitter as the director strides away.

Franz

The rest of rehearsal crawls by at a snail's pace. Every passing minute lasts an hour; every hour takes a whole fucking year. Somehow, someway, we get through another three scenes, and I scramble enough of my brain cells to give the actors decent notes, even when Sylvie keeps looking at me like *that*.

Smiling shyly. Twisting her fingers in her lap, or tucking her blonde hair behind her ears. Blushing and sweet and eager.

Can't believe she didn't know that I wanted her. Can't believe she doubted this. I figured it's been painfully obvious, so clear that the stage manager gives me knowing looks every time he comes to discuss tech for the show, and I've been stewing this whole time about whether I've been making my girl uncomfortable.

I've been trying to rein it *in*. Trying to keep my distance and let her breathe.

And all along, Sylvie's been thinking I don't want her at all. Christ, I could slam my head against a wall. For an ostensibly intelligent man, I can be a complete idiot.

"Great work today."

By the time rehearsal comes to an end, my nerves are frayed to oblivion. I'm hanging by my last damn thread, because Sylvie keeps staring at me and wetting her lips, and I don't care if it's obvious and everyone in the cast will gossip. Don't care if they think I'm too old for her. Don't care about being careful anymore.

Sylvie said she wants me. She got sad when she thought I didn't feel the same way.

So this is happening. A charging wild bull couldn't stop me at this point.

"Go over your lines for Act Four, please, and make sure you stretch out if you fought today. Take care of your bodies, because we need everyone well rested for opening night."

My words spill out of me on autopilot, but I can't look away from Sylvie. Can't even bring myself to scan the room, to see everyone else whispering and wide-eyed about how obvious I'm being. Who cares?

Sylvie wants me. That's what she said.

Will she come to me now? Is she finally ready?

The actors all file out of the auditorium, chatting together and smothering bursts of laughter. That's fine. They can gossip; they can tease. If Sylvie comes to me like she promised, I'll shout that fact to the rooftops myself.

My girl sits there now, blushing but resolute in her blue velvet seat. Waiting while everyone else packs up and leaves one by one, stuffing their belongings in backpacks and fishing under their chairs for lost water bottles. If these students move any slower, I'll light a fire just to chase them out of here.

Sylvie.

When the door slams closed behind the last actor, when their voices echo away down distant halls, we're left in an empty auditorium all alone. The air is thick, and Sylvie presses her lips together, watching me in silence. Those big blue eyes urge me to *do* something, to take the pressure off her somehow, and god, I'd do anything for this young woman.

"Come here. Come with me." My hand stretches out toward her, and Sylvie blows out a relieved breath and smiles. She stands, slinging her backpack over her shoulders, then edges her way to the end of the row.

I meet her in the aisle, taking her hand. Her fingers are so soft and delicate compared to mine, and I grip her carefully, suddenly afraid to hurt her.

"This way."

The wooden steps up to the stage creak beneath our shared weight, declaring loudly to anyone nearby that we're still here, that we're sneaking off together. Sylvie giggles nervously, and I squeeze her fingers in response.

She's mine.

This is really happening. Sylvie is coming with me.

The stage is empty, and there are shadowy pools of darkness in both wings. The flies soar high overhead, ghostly pieces of set hanging up there in the gloom, while the blue velvet seats behind us are silent and watchful, waiting for their next audience.

A distant thump echoes in the silence. There's the judder of a drill. Someone's in the workshop, working on the set.

That's fine. We veer in the opposite direction, slipping into the wings on stage right, where the air smells like old fabric and hot lights. The familiar scent of the theater.

"Where are we going?" Sylvie whispers, clinging to my

hand like it's her personal lifeline. She follows behind me, so close that she keeps stepping on the backs of my shoes and apologizing.

I don't care. I *want* her close, even if it makes us both clumsy. Every inch between our bodies is an inch too far, and I'll demonstrate that fact shortly.

"You'll see in a moment." Once her eyes adjust to the gloom, anyway, because there are no working lights backstage right now. No one around but us.

Just as well, really. Now that I've finally gotten my girl alone, I don't want to hold back. Not for anything in the world.

Our footsteps scuff against the floor. Heavy black drapes hang all around, soaking up the sound, and it's like I'm leading her deeper into the labyrinth.

She wants this, I remind myself for the hundredth time. *It's okay.*

The piece of scenery is right where I left it after inspecting it this morning, pushed back against the wall in the stage right wing. Juliet's balcony is level with my chest, twined in ivy and guarded on both corners by stone statues of lions. Eventually, there will be a wrought iron railing to keep the actors from falling off, but for now…

Sylvie sucks in a breath as I lift her up, sitting her gently on the balcony's edge. Her knees tremble where they nudge against my chest, and Sylvie grips my shoulders so tight her fingernails dig into the muscle.

"What are you doing?" she hisses, but there's a delighted smile playing around her mouth. "Franz!"

"Relax." Stroking two palms up her thighs, I groan quietly when Sylvie melts and parts her legs for me automatically. So responsive. So *sweet*. What would she be like in bed, not having

171

to sneak around and whisper? Would she cry out? Would she beg? If I don't find out soon, I'll go insane. "I won't let you fall, sweetheart. Trust me."

Fingertips drift across my cheekbone, tracing the contours of my face. "I do," Sylvie confesses quietly. "I do trust you. But I still don't know why you want me up here—"

My head ducks down in answer, because screw that. Screw Sylvie being unsure, looking at me like I might change my mind any minute. My mouth skims up the length of her leggings-clad thigh, until I'm breathing directly against her pussy, misting it through the fabric, my breaths already ragged with hunger. Is that answer enough?

"Oh," Sylvie says faintly, even as her fingers weave through my hair and *tug*. The prickle of pain feels so good, centering me. "Oh, that."

"Yes." My words rumble against her clit through her leggings, and Sylvie squirms, pushing her hips toward me, already eager for more contact. "*That.*"

There's no one around. No one to hear the whisper of fabric as I tease her leggings down her thighs; no one to catch a glimpse of creamy bare skin in the gloom. Sylvie's not wearing any underwear beneath her leggings, and that knowledge spears into my brain like a red-hot lance.

Mine.

Need to touch her. Need to taste her.

Need to feel her squirm and writhe.

Need to work this angel into a panting, sweaty mess, until she hungers for me with the same desperation I feel for her. Need to ruin Sylvie for all other men, and claim her forever.

Then I can breathe again. Nothing else will do.

"Never thought I'd get a turn on this balcony," Sylvie jokes weakly, scratching at my scalp. Her breath hitches when I lean forward again, trailing open mouthed kisses up her inner thigh. Her legs are thick and curvy, just like the rest of her, and I want to stroke my hands over every single inch of this perfect body.

"You're *my* Juliet." I press the words against her pussy like an offering, like a prayer, and the salty-sweet tang of her musk flips a switch in my brain. There's no other way to describe it: I get the tiniest taste of her, then primal instinct takes over.

Because Sylvie's legs are spread, her taste is on my tongue, and she is *mine*. Mine to kiss and knead and worship.

Mouth twisting in a snarl, I lick a stripe up Sylvie's slit.

"Oo-oh!" The balcony creaks as Sylvie leans back, tugging me closer by the hair. She's panting already, her hips rocking up to meet my tongue, and I *knew* she'd like this. Knew she'd make the best little noises. "Oh, god. Okay. That feels so— *Franz*."

Is there any sweeter sound than my name on her lips? Especially when she says it like *that*, all needy and breathless. My heart lurches in response, and I angle my head, lapping at her clit.

"This is so crazy." Fingernails scratch at my scalp, and Sylvie strokes my neck, then my shoulders, gripping hard to the bunched muscle there. "Is this really happening?"

Oh, it's happening alright—and let there be no doubt about it. Tearing my mouth away, I tell her: "Don't you doubt it, sweetheart. This is my tongue on your pussy. This is us in this wing. Feel this?"

Sylvie's mouth drops open as I slide a finger inside her, breaching her tight channel. It's slick and soft and blissfully warm, and it's going to feel like heaven around my cock. But in the meantime...

"That's me touching you, Sylvie. *Claiming* you. Has anyone ever touched you here before?"

She makes a muffled sound, shaking her head. Didn't think so. She's too tight, too shy, too innocent. And I'm so fucking glad to be her first, even if that makes me a caveman, because no other man in the world could ever worship her like I will. No other would fully appreciate this prize.

Molten desire simmers in my veins.

When I bury my face between Sylvie's legs again, two soft thighs clamp around my head like earmuffs. And I sure hope Sylvie's listening out for people coming near, because I can't hear a damn thing anymore—only the rush of blood in my ears. My jaw clicks but I keep licking; my neck aches but I crane closer. This wing is hot and dark and dusty, but this is better than any theoretical feather bed because this is *real.* Sylvie is mine, and my chin is glossy with her sheen.

"*Franz.*"

With those gorgeous thighs squeezing my ears, her voice sounds like it's coming from far, far away. But I hear it, just like I sense the wave of tension rippling through her body, and feel her bare skin flash even hotter. Sylvie bucks and moans and writhes on my finger, and I don't let up for a single second. Not until she freezes, breath held—then falls apart on Juliet's balcony.

She comes silently, one hand clapped over her mouth, her eyes locked on mine the whole time. She's a work of art.

And when I finally straighten up, neck aching, and wipe my mouth with the back of my wrist...

Sylvie grins at me.

And I fall impossibly harder.

174

Sylvie

～◦◦◦～

L et it be known: the rumors are true. Sneaking around backstage *is* super fun. For the next two weeks until opening night, Franz and I try out every shadowy corner and disused dressing room we can find.

Not during rehearsals, obviously. When we're on the clock, Franz is serious as hell about his job, pacing back and forth below the stage and making endless notes for the actors. He works with the designers to find the perfect lights, set and costumes, and as opening night draws closer, he works longer and longer hours, trying to make sure everything is perfect.

It's sweet, really. This man is a world-renowned director, working on this college production as a favor to his old friend, our Dean. *The* Franz Moser could put barely any effort in to this show and still be heaped with praise, but instead he's drilling us all like we're all professionals on London's West End. Trying to give us an amazing experience.

It's thrilling. Exhausting.

And so freaking sexy.

Apparently there *is* something hotter than a stern older man—and it's a stern older man who clearly needs a nap. Seriously, what has broken in my brain?

"Sylvie?" Franz glances up when I slip inside the auditorium at ten to midnight, dressed in his gray sweater and frayed denim shorts. We're deep into spring now, and it was hot and sunny all day, but the nighttime chill has left goosebumps all over my bare thighs. "It's late. What are you doing here?"

The director is puzzled but pleased. As though there was a serious chance that I might not come to him tonight; as though I could go a full twenty four hours without his lips at my throat. Usually, yeah, we've been finding chances to sneak off during the day, but today was our last full day of rehearsal, and Franz hasn't had a single spare minute. I've *missed* him.

The strain of directing shows on his handsome face as I stroll along his row in the auditorium. The lines are etched deeper at the corner of his eyes, and Franz stares at me like I'm an oasis in the desert.

"You work too hard," I say.

His mouth quirks up, and damn—that daily stubble is dark as hell. Bet if I chafe my palm against it, it'll be in full sandpaper mode. I shove my hands in my shorts pockets instead, coming to stand a few seats away.

Like always, my chest throbs with the need to be closer, *closer*. In this man's lap; in his arms. Hearing him grunt and groan and mutter my name over and over like a prayer, kissing me and stroking me like I'm the best thing he's ever seen.

It still doesn't feel real. After two full weeks of having Franz Moser be openly obsessed with me, not caring at all who sees him take my hand or nuzzle my cheek, you'd think I could trust this by now. You'd think I'd be settling in, loosening up, and enjoying every minute. And yet... somehow, this all feels too good to be true.

Because I'm the understudy, you know? The eternal second choice. The shy, curvy girl who can never seem to land a leading role, and now this wolfishly handsome director is supposedly super into me? Make sense of *that*.

"You're tired," Franz murmurs, holding out a hand. When I take it, he tugs me down into his lap, wrapping his arms around me and resting his chin on my shoulder. Sandpaper stubble: confirmed.

"Pot, kettle, black," I say.

Franz huffs a laugh and kisses my neck.

And this is *nice*. It's so freaking nice, and my insides go all tingly whenever this man is near. So why can't I trust that this is real? Why can't I finally relax and enjoy it? Why is a secret part of me still clenched with nerves, waiting for the other shoe to drop?

Maybe because Franz hasn't slept with me yet. He's kissed me and touched me and tasted me *down there* more time than I can count, but he's never once pushed for more. Why not? Doesn't he want to?

Or maybe because tomorrow is opening night—and once the play launches, there's no reason for Franz to stay in Kephart any longer. He'll go back to London, back to his big, fancy career in the West End, and he hasn't mentioned the words 'long distance' to me once. Hasn't hinted at all that I could come and visit him. Will this be over before it's even begun? Won't he fuck me even once before he goes?

"Growing up in Vienna, my mother always told me not to trust late night troubles." Warm breath tickles my neck, before Franz's teeth gently scrape my earlobe. "Whatever it is, whatever is troubling you, Liebe—it won't seem so terrible in the morning. Our worries shrink back to size with the sunrise."

Yeah… except my worries come closer with the dawn, too. Because tomorrow is opening night, and what then?

Ask him. Ask him, you coward.

But my tongue stays resolutely glued to the roof of my mouth, and I play with Franz's collar instead. He's wearing a wine red button-down shirt today, the sleeves rolled, and his brown eyes are just about the most beautiful sight I've ever seen. Like rich milk chocolate, flecked with gold.

"Liebe?"

His smile curves up. "It means love."

My toes curl in my sneakers, and I turn to stare dry-eyed at the empty stage. A spotlight shines down on the scenery for the opening scene, and someone's dropped a prop near the stage left wing. Some kind of paper scroll, maybe.

"I'll miss you." The words burst out of me in a rush, and it's not exactly what I wanted to tell this man, but it's not wrong either. Can't look at him, but I need to get this out, because it's been festering inside me worse and worse each day. "After tomorrow, I'll miss you so much."

There's a long pause behind me, Franz's arms tightening around my waist. The strap of his expensive watch digs into my ribs, ticking down the minutes until midnight, and Franz is right: it *is* getting late, and I still have assignments to work on tonight. But I couldn't stay away. The thought of a whole day without Franz's arms around me? It's unthinkable.

My heart plummets when Franz rasps, "Me too."

It's not what I wanted to hear from him… but it'll have to do.

* * *

Opening night is hectic as hell. The stage manager prowls around backstage, dressed all in black with a buzzing headset, searching for lost props and double checking all the tech. Dressers sew last minute tears in costumes, whispering apologies when they prick the actors with needles, and the dressing rooms are a constant hum of nervous conversation.

I'm huddled in the corner, lacing into my ensemble costume. It's one of those buxom peasant dresses with the criss-cross laces over my boobs, and every time Franz sees me in it, his expression sharpens. So I don't mind the costume really, don't mind having such a small role when the pressure tonight is sky-high, but a deep voice calls to me from the doorway before I can finish getting ready.

"Franz?" I push outside, the temperature dropping away from the press of bodies. "I'm nearly done."

The dressing room door swings shut behind me as I gaze up at the director in the hallway. Franz is dressed in a soft black sweater that hugs the muscled planes of his chest, and his jaw is freshly shaved for tonight's occasion. He *should* be all business right now, doing any final checks before the curtain goes up, but instead he's staring down at me with a funny look on his face.

"Franz?"

"Loren has a family emergency," he rasps. "You're up, Liebe. You're playing Juliet tonight."

My stomach swoops like I'm riding a roller coaster. Me? I'm playing Juliet *tonight*?

"Are you serious?"

Franz's eyes crinkle when he smiles, but he can't hide the tension in his shoulders. "That would be a very unfunny joke."

It really would. And I know I've been preparing for this,

I know that I have Juliet's lines memorized, but a cold chill still sweeps down my spine. Because… what if I'm not good enough? What if I ruin the show for everyone else? What if Franz sees me onstage making a mess of things, and then doesn't even bother saying goodbye?

"There, there," the director murmurs, spinning me around to rub my shoulders. "It's normal to be nervous, especially when you didn't expect to go onstage tonight. But you *are* ready for this, Sylvie. You are a leading lady, and you're going to prove that to everyone."

A dresser rushes past in the narrow hallway, the costume she's carrying brushing our legs. She glances at us as she hurries past, but she doesn't even blink when she finds *the* Franz Moser nuzzling my temple and giving me a pep talk, because over the last two weeks, *everyone* has seen us together.

Everyone knows this man is into me. That my super embarrassing, radioactive crush was requited all along. That thought squares my shoulders, and I raise my chin.

"I can do this," I declare to the empty air, and Franz hums with approval, kissing my jaw. His soap and cedar scent is all around me, soothing my nerves and heating up my insides at the same time, and I love him, I love him, I love him.

I don't *want* to let him go. Don't want to say goodbye to this man. The thought of it makes me feel like I'm splitting in two.

And if I'm brave enough to go onstage as Juliet tonight, I'm brave enough to confess how I feel.

"I don't want you to leave after this." My words are shaky, but I force them out anyway. Even if it makes me sound like a naive idiot; even if I'm offering up my heart to get trampled. "I know you need to go back to London, but I'm just saying—I don't want that. I'll miss you every day. And I hope… I hope

I can come to visit you there soon. Maybe in the summer. If you'd want that."

Franz is statue-still behind me, his grip rigid on my shoulders. His lips have frozen at my throat, and I swear I can *feel* the tension vibrating inside him.

"I don't want that," he grits out at last.

Oh, *god*.

My heart shrivels in my chest. My cheeks flush hot and my throat goes tight, and I try to shrug him off, try to run off and bawl my eyes out into the nearest drape, but Franz won't let me, holding me too tight.

"I don't want that," he says again, his grip firm on me, "because I don't want a *visit* from you, Liebe. I don't want to be parted from you for a single day. If you'll let me, I'll stay here with you in Kephart until you finish your studies. *Then* we can go to London together, or wherever else you like. Don't you understand by now, Sylvie? *This* is what I want. *You*."

...Oh. Guess I'd better stop trying to elbow him in the stomach.

I clear my throat, feeling a dizzy mix of pure, soaring joy and complete embarrassment.

"But we haven't even... you haven't want to... you know."

Franz's dark chuckle makes my nipples harden against my dress. "Haven't I? Haven't I wanted that?"

With a single yank, he pulls me fully against his body, pressed flush so I can feel his muscled chest and toned stomach and— and the hard line of his cock digging into my lower back.

"Patience is not the same thing as disinterest, Sylvie. I didn't want to push you too fast. But have no doubt: I *will* claim you that way—and now that I know you're eager, I'll do it before the night's end."

My head swims. Footsteps echo along the corridor, coming our way, and Franz reluctantly allows a few inches between our bodies, nodding over my head at the sound tech as he walks past.

"Really?" I whisper once we're alone again. This has all been a lot to take in, and I'm woozy with nerves and excitement about all of it. Playing Juliet tonight; having Franz stay in Kephart for me; the rough catch in his voice when he promised we'll do *that* in the next few hours. No wonder I'm bright pink and breathing hard.

"Really." Sharp teeth nip my earlobe, then I'm nudged back toward the dressing room. "Break a leg, Liebe."

Franz

Nerves squirm in my stomach as I settle into my seat in the front row. As the director, it's my job not to let any uncertainties show. But the truth is, opening night is always hard. What if I've misjudged this performance? What if the actors aren't ready?

What if, what if, what if.

In theory, I should be less nervous about this college production than a professional show on the West End. But in reality, this is even worse. These are precious hopes and dreams I'm shepherding, young actors at the very beginning of their careers, and as I glance back and forth at the audience around me, my hackles are raised. Though I don't let any emotion cross my face, I *feel* fiercely protective of my students.

Then there's Sylvie.

My Juliet.

Ever since the first week of rehearsals, she's been the true lead in my mind—even as I gave Loren my full encouragement. It was too late to swap their roles, and I'd never admit this out loud, but I'm privately glad that it's Sylvie up there tonight instead.

She deserves this. The limelight; the applause. The chance to show the world what she can do. The chance for everyone else to see her as *I* do: as beautiful, talented, charming.

A woman next to me flicks through the playbill, chatting quietly with her friend. On my other side, a man scrolls through his phone until he catches my side-eye and switches it off. When I turn around, the whole auditorium is packed, every blue velvet seat filled, and the whole room buzzes with excited energy.

Sylvie.

My nerves settle as I turn back around, getting comfortable in my chair. The lights dim, and the curtain sweeps up.

It's her moment.

* * *

Two hours later, I'm on my feet with the rest of the audience, clapping so hard my hands are going numb. Someone whistles in the row behind me; the woman next to me is hopping up and down, waving at someone onstage. The actors beam out into the bright stage lights, taking another bow before filing away into the wings.

They were good. No—great. Despite a couple of fudged lines and one forgotten prop, all of which they smoothed over so the audience didn't notice, they brought the damn house down.

And Sylvie... *Sylvie.*

After tonight, I'm surer than ever: my Liebe is a star in the making.

The audience takes an age to collect their things and file out into the perfumed spring night. I stand and wait impatiently, tapping my foot and checking my watch, all too desperate to get backstage again. When the woman in front of me stops to tie her shoe lace, I choke back a frustrated growl, and when I finally reach the aisle, I practically fly across the auditorium and out of the side door.

So many winding corridors backstage. So many prop stores and drape cupboards and harried-looking dressers, bustling back and forth with costumes draped over their arms. I weave my way through all of it, murmuring congratulations and offering smiles to jittery actors, but there's only one person I really want to see.

The ladies dressing room is buzzing and loud when I reach it. Rapping on the door with my knuckles, I step back in the hallway and wait.

One of the ensemble sticks her head through the doorway, sees me, and snorts. She ducks back inside, and I can't help grinning as she calls Sylvie's name.

Of course everyone knows why I'm here. I've never hidden the way I feel about Sylvie, not really. Frankly, it seemed an impossible task.

She's *mine*. And I'm hers. Behaving otherwise is unthinkable.

My jagged heartbeat finally settles when Sylvie flies through the doorway and into my arms.

"Franz! Oh my god. Did you see it? Were you watching?"

"Of course I was watching." Her blonde hair smells of hairspray when I nuzzle it, and she's definitely smudging stage makeup on my sweater, but I don't care. I *want* Sylvie's marks on me. Want her close, especially when she's thrumming with excitement like this. What's a little extra laundry? "You were perfect."

She lunges up and kisses me, a smile curving against my mouth.

And there are people all around, chattering excitedly and swapping gossip. This whole theater is crawling with people right now, and will be for the next thirty minutes at least. But if there's one thing Sylvie and I have learned over the last two weeks, it's all the best spots to sneak away and hide backstage.

"Come on."

Sylvie lets me tug her along the hallway, her giggles soft and sweet. She's changed out of her Juliet costume into a pair of shorts and a pink t-shirt, and she's wearing sneakers that squeak quietly against the linoleum floor.

Posters line the walls—old Kephart college productions. How many of those was Sylvie in? There are still so many things I need to ask her; so many things I need to know. I'll never get tired of this young woman, will never have enough of her to sate my hunger, but for now...

I test the door handle to a disused dressing room. We already snuck away here for a few minutes alone last week, but I still breathe out a sigh of relief when the handle turns.

"So glamorous," Sylvie teases, entering first and flicking a light switch. Bulbs studded around a big mirror blaze to life, casting the dressing room in a warm glow.

"I'll take you to a luxury suite after this," I promise, shutting the door behind me and flipping the lock. We're deep enough in the building here that all the backstage ruckus has faded to a faint buzz. "Rose petals on the bed, a huge bathtub, champagne on the balcony. The works."

Sylvie laughs, hopping up to sit on the table in front of the lit-up mirror. "I'm not sure, Mr Moser. I kinda like all this sneaking around. Besides, Kephart isn't really that sort of town."

It could be, though. If that's what Sylvie wanted, if it would make her happy, I'd find a way to make it happen. I'm a director, after all. I'm used to creating something out of nothing.

"I bet you miss London." Sylvie holds up her arms, and I go to stand in front of her, nudging her knees apart with my hips. She winds her arms around my neck and presses up against me, her softness to my hard chest, and Christ, I will never tire of this feeling. "Bet you miss the big city."

"Not really."

It's hard to miss anything when I'm with Sylvie. Something deep inside me knows: this is exactly where I ought to be.

"But you'd like it there," I say. "And you could audition for roles on the West End."

Sylvie laughs, her excitement so warm and bright, before tugging me down for a long, deep kiss.

The rest of the world fades away. Time and space—all of it. There's nothing except Sylvie's eager mouth on mine, and our tongues sliding together, and the urgent throb of both our bodies. Need to get closer. Need to get *in*.

I tear my mouth away, heaving for breath. Sylvie's worked up too, she's red-cheeked and clumsy as she yanks her t-shirt over her head, and my heart drums as I follow with my own sweater flung at the wall.

We shed layers like we can't breathe until we're naked, tearing seams and kicking shoes so hard they bounce into the dressing room corners. And then we're clasped together, bare skin against bare skin, our bodies blurring together in the mirror behind Sylvie.

Her thighs spread, welcoming me closer. My shaft slides

along her pink, slick pussy, feeling how ready she is for me. Swollen and wanting. How she quivers at my smallest touch.
Sylvie.

The sound she makes when I pinch her nipples is the sweetest torture. Seared into my brain. And when I press a finger inside her, teasing her nerve endings and coaxing her to soften...

Sylvie stiffens at first, her breath puffing against my neck... then she *melts.* My groan of approval echoes around the empty dressing room, and my fingers are glossy as I pump them between her legs.

"You're tight," I murmur, mouth pressed against her temple, fingertips stroking inside her perfect body. Sylvie shudders. "You're tight, but you're going to open for me, aren't you, Liebe? You're going to let me in. You're going to let me thrust deep where I belong."

Sylvie hiccups and nods.

She claws at my back as I line up with her entrance; she bites my shoulder as I nudge the first inch inside. And though she tenses up at first, her lower back damp beneath my palm, after a minute of stroking and soothing and kissing her with shameless hunger... Sylvie softens for me.

"Christ." Jaw clenched, I work my way deeper. *Deeper.* Swiveling my hips, burrowing my way inside, and the knowledge that I'm her first and only makes me want to beat my chest and howl. "Do you know how good you feel, Sylvie? How perfect you are? Jesus Christ, I'm going to blow."

She makes the sweetest sound—half laugh, half moan—and wriggles her hips when I pause to catch my breath, trying to make sure I don't lose control way too soon.

She just feels so good, so *right.* And every instinct inside me screams to thrust deep and pound until her teeth clack together, then fill her up with my seed. And I'll do that, I will, but first I'll be a gentleman, damn it. I *need* her to like this too, because I already know that without it I'll die.

"Stop wriggling. You're going to make me—*stop*."

Sylvie does not listen. If anything, she wriggles more, the beautiful brat, biting her plump lower lip. When I spank the side of her ass, the sound cracking through the quiet dressing room, Sylvie moans in shameless triumph.

A gush of wetness over the head of my cock tells me everything I need to know. My girl loved that. She likes me stern; likes me bossy.

And she's ready to take whatever I want to give her.

The final thread of my control snaps.

Sylvie

~∞~

The second Franz's palm smacks against my ass, a wave of molten heat rushes through my whole body. *Yes.*

This is what I want: Franz in control, taking care of business. Taking care of *me.* Maybe not in every aspect of our lives together, but in this? These moments when he lays siege to my body and makes me gasp and moan and whimper? These moments when he presses inside me like he owns me?

Hell yes, I want it like this. And I let him know by scratching my fingernails down his back, tilting my hips up in offering, and groaning happily when he thrusts another few inches inside.

"You're mine," Franz mutters, thrusting steadily now, feeding me his full length with each pump of his hips. There's a faint sting from his intrusion, a pleasant sort of ache, but mostly it feels so good that my eyes nearly cross. "You're mine. Say it, Sylvie."

"I'm yours." My words are faint, breathless, but I know he hears me because there's a rumbling sound in his chest, and

190

then Franz spreads my thighs wider and pounds mercilessly between them. My boobs jiggle as the table creaks beneath us, but I don't care, okay? I don't care.

Don't care if this dressing room is nothing but rubble when we leave it. Don't care if Franz can see *all* of my squishiest bits right now, aided by the mirror, because he's searing me with his hungry gaze. There's no chance to feel self conscious.

This man loves my curves. He's *starving* for them.

And as far as I'm concerned, they're all his. The director's personal playground.

Tension squirms in my belly, ratcheting tighter with every thrust. When Franz presses his thumb against my clit and starts rubbing steady circles, I tip my head back with a tortured groan. And I'm sweaty and flushed and the wet noises where our bodies meet are so obscene, but I love every single thing about this.

Love the way he owns me, surrounds me, *conquers* me with every thrust.

Love the frayed expression in his brown eyes—half need, half reverence.

And I love when his teeth scrape my throat, and Franz snarls against my skin: "Come for me, Liebe. Come on my cock. Show me how sweet you can be."

His command is what pushes me over the edge. That, and his thumb on my clit and his fierce grip in my hair, his heat, his scent, the stretch of him pushing rhythmically inside me. My eyes squeeze shut and my toes curl behind his back, and Franz rumbles in approval as I fall apart with a squeak.

"*Yes*," he groans, his movements getting jerky. Sloppy. "Yes, that's it. Christ, that's it. I can feel you, Liebchen. Twitching and grasping. Can feel you milking me."

My whole body is on fire.

And the pleasure is so intense, it's almost too much to bear. So much that I don't notice Franz coming too at first, until the warmth of his come spills out of me onto the table below in a sticky *drip, drip, drip.*

Franz keeps thrusting anyway, pushing his seed deeper inside me. Muttering about how he loves me, how perfect I am, how I'm built for his cock, and how he'll put me on my hands and knees every day and make me scream. How he knows how to worship me right.

This is insane.

This is the best day of my whole freaking life.

As our breaths even out and the sweat cools on our skin, Franz tucks a lock of hair behind my ear and smiles sheepishly. I poke my tongue out back at him, all jangled up and so, so alive.

And you know what? There's no need for him to worry or look sheepish.

Because the things he promised—they're exactly what I want too.

* * *

Five years later

My head drops back and I groan at the ceiling, my play script crumpled in my lap. Shakespeare, man. This stuff doesn't get any easier to learn. And the fact that I'm playing Helena in A Midsummer Night's Dream—one of my favorite ever roles, in one of the best theaters in London too—well, that doesn't help with the pressure.

I'm nervous. No way around it. Because what if I screw this role up? What if my career is over before it begins? What if my daughter grows up to think of her mother as a failed actor?

Oh, god. I should have studied finance or something. Why do I keep letting Franz convince me I can do this?

The front door to the apartment opens behind me. "We're back," my husband calls, striding into the room with our toddler balanced on his hip. She's dressed up for summer in dungarees and a cute little bucket hat, sunscreen streaked across her cheeks and nose, and she blinks at me with familiar brown eyes then reaches for me without a word.

"Oh, dear." Franz waits for me to stand from the sofa, then hands her over cheerfully. "Looks like I'm out of fashion already. She wants her mother. Well, she can have five minutes and then it's bath time."

"Five minutes," I whisper into my daughter's wispy hair. She cuddles my neck, and her hands have that tell-tale stickiness that says they got ice cream. "Five minutes of cuddles, then Mommy has to learn this stupid play."

"That's the attitude." Franz sounds amused, picking up empty mugs and ferrying them through to the kitchen. "This will make your career, but yes, it's very stupid."

Just like that, the pressure wells up in me and closes my throat. Breathing steadily, I cuddle my daughter close and try not to freak out.

But Franz must sense his mistake, because a minute late our toddler is plucked from my arms. She squirms a little but she must be sleepy too, because she doesn't fight when he carries her off into her bedroom, declaring that it's nap time.

Then strong arms wind around my waist from behind, and I'm marched to the big windows overlooking our tree-dotted borough of London. Warm breath mists my neck, and my husband kisses along my jaw.

"Freaking out?" Franz murmurs, humming when I nod. "There's no need, Liebe. You're going to be wonderful in this role, just like you are in every play."

My lips press together, and I pluck at his sleeve. He's wearing the gray sweater that he draped me in all those years ago, and the sight of it always settles me.

"What if I'm not?" I whisper. "What if I bomb, and then I never get another role again? Would you still...?"

My question trails off, too embarrassingly needy for me to say it out loud. But Franz must hear the unspoken words, because he chuckles and squeezes me tighter.

"I would love you even if you were the worst actor in the world," he declares. "Even if you wore a potato sack every day and ate only celery. Even if you broke out in giant red pustules. Even if—"

"Okay, I get the picture." I pat his wrist, feeling weirdly better, then spin around in my husband's arms. "Thank you."

Franz gazes down at me, his handsome face etched with love. There's a little more silver in his temples, but otherwise he's the same man I fell for all those years ago back in Kephart. He's still just as hungry for me too, like he'll never get enough of me, even if we spend the rest of our lives together.

"Sooo..." I bite my lip, smoothing my palms over Franz's sturdy chest. This sweater always gets me all tingly and ready. "She's down for a nap?"

His mouth curves up, his eyes heating. "Out like a light. I'd say we have a few stolen moments."

That's all we need. That's all we've *ever* needed.

After all: sneaking around together is fun as hell.

Sylvie

* * *

Thanks for reading the Practice Makes Perfect series! I hope you liked it. :)

For more star-crossed couples at Kephart College, check out the Crossed Lines box set, starting with The Shrink. *They sent me to therapy against my will. But since I met my therapist, whole armies couldn't keep me away.*

Happy reading!

xxx

Teaser: The Shrink

"So." The man steeples his fingers, elbows resting on the desk. He watches me across the expanse. "Tell me why you are here."

Um.

"Are–are you sure?" I jab a thumb at the set up behind me. There's a classic brown leather therapist's couch facing a hard-looking chair, with a side table and a box of tissues between them. It's way more inviting than this desk, and more what I pictured from a therapy session. Sitting here, I feel like I'm in trouble.

Which, okay, I guess I kind of am. "Shouldn't we sit over there?"

"No." A tiny smile ghosts across the man's face. "This will be fine for today. Now: why are you here, Kennedy?"

"You know my name," I say dumbly. The hairs rise on the back of my neck. It's *weird*, sitting here with this cool, calm stranger who watches me so closely and already knows my name. Especially since I keep forgetting *his*.

Smith, or something. Sotherby. Steele. Something beginning with 's'.

He doesn't look how I expected. I pictured a doddery old

man, or a middle aged woman draped in shawls. This guy, with his dark beard and piercing blue eyes and broad shoulders under his white shirt–he's kind of unsettling.

"I read your details when you were referred to me."

'Referred' is such a gentle way of putting it. 'Bundled here against my will' is more like it. But–

"So you already know why I'm here," I say flatly. God, I've only been here two minutes and it's like riddling with a sphinx. "You don't need me to tell you."

That faint, flitting smile again. "Nonetheless. I'd like to hear your perspective."

How generous. I shift in my chair, mouth clamped shut, and wow, normally no one can get me to shut up. I'm annoyingly chatty, always running my mouth, yet in this room with this man, I suddenly don't want to say a word.

"You're nervous," the man announces. "Why?"

I clear my throat. I can do this. "I don't want to say the wrong thing."

He nods, eyes on me. "There is no wrong thing."

"Yes, there is."

He waits.

And waits.

Damn him.

"If I say the wrong thing, you'll tell my parents," I blurt. "They sent me here. They're paying for this." I may be twenty one years old, a fully grown woman, but I made the mistake of letting my overly controlling parents pay my tuition. I'll still be dancing to their tune for another year–if I want to finish my degree, anyway.

Some days that feels more worth it than others.

"I don't report on my sessions," the man says, his voice calm and deep. "Unless you plan on confessing to a crime, nothing you say will leave this room."

A crime. Okay. Does that include climbing out of my dorm window in the middle of the night? It broke campus rules, sure, but the law?

I guess I did damage that window screen. Shit.

"Your late night adventure does not warrant a call to the police." The man's mouth twitches. "In case you were wondering."

I splutter. This asshole! Sitting there, with his bottomless gaze and his stupid sexy beard and his bookcase of fancy leather hardbacks behind him. I bet he doesn't even read them. "See, you *do* know. You know everything already."

The man hums. *Dr Sterling*, I remember suddenly. It's a sharp name. It suits him.

"I don't know the most important thing, Kennedy. I don't know *why*."

Ah, yeah. Why did I break that window screen by scrambling out of my second floor bedroom at 2am and jumping into a tree? Why did I climb down in the old, baggy t-shirt and sweatpants I wear for pajamas, then set off to wander around campus like a ghost?

If I knew, maybe I'd tell him.

"Why does anyone do anything?" I say airily, leaning back in my chair. Maybe I can bullshit my way through these sessions. "Don't you ever do something impulsive, Dr Sterling?"

"Rarely." He tilts his head, still staring, and my attempt to flip things around has failed miserably. I'm a fly under his microscope. "But this is not about me."

I wish it wasn't about me, either. I'm chatty out there in the real world, sure, but not about my private shit. I don't bare my soul to any passing stranger. No one would know anything about my secret late night jaunts if campus security hadn't caught me.

"Your parents are worried about you," Dr Sterling offers.

I snort. "Try again."

He keeps talking like I never spoke. "Should they be, Kennedy? Should people be worried about you?"

What a question. *Should people be worried about me?*

I mean, sure. In a general sense. Maybe it's needy of me, but I'd like to feel a modicum of concern from someone out there. But my parents?

"Nope. I'm good, thank you."

Dr Sterling nods, expression thoughtful. "And yet you are committed to these sessions."

"I don't have a whole lot of choice in the matter."

"Indeed."

The silence stretches between us, punctuated by the *tick, tick, tick* of the small clock resting on the bookcase. I point over his shoulder. "Do you ever read those?"

Dr Sterling smiles. "Sometimes."

"And why did you want to be a therapist?"

His smile widens. "I'm not sure you understand how this works, Kennedy."

Oh, I understand alright. This guy gets paid a boatload of money to sit there and–and *pry*. To tease out my secrets and then judge me for them. No thank you, mister.

"What's the weirdest problem you've ever heard?"

Tick, tick, tick goes the clock. Counting down this endless session. Dr Sterling sighs and settles deeper into his chair, plucking a pen off the desk and rolling it between his fingers, and it's like he finally realizes that this is going to suck for him, too. I won't come easy, damn it. He'll never take me alive!

"I am very clearly not going to divulge that information."

I guess not. And whatever it is, I get this weird, swooping urge to beat it—to offer him something even more bat-shit crazy to refuse to tell anyone else. If only my life was more exciting... but I'll try.

"I got attacked by an alpaca once, at a petting zoo as a kid. It charged me down, right in front of the other preschoolers."

A short pause. Then—

"Fine." Dr Sterling tosses his pen onto the desk and leans forward, pinning me with those stern eyes. I shift in my seat, shivers rippling up my limbs.

Oh god, that *stare.* Those shoulders. The rich timbre of his voice. This man is so potent, he could be weaponized. Whole nations would kneel at his feet.

"You win, Kennedy. Let's start with the alpaca."

* * *

Check out The Shrink, or go straight to Crossed Lines, the Kephart College complete series box set!

xxx

200

Cassie Mint

About the Author

Cassie writes outrageous, OTT insta-love with tons of sugar and spice. She loves cookie dough, summer barbecues, and her gorgeous cat Missy.

You can connect with me on:
🌐 https://www.authorcassiemint.com
f https://www.facebook.com/cassiemintauthor
🔗 https://www.bookbub.com/authors/cassie-mint

Subscribe to my newsletter:
✉ https://www.authorcassiemint.com/newsletter